GUY OF WARWICK
AND OTHER CHAPBOOK ROMANCES

The editor: John Simons is Professor and Head of the
School of Humanities and Arts at Edge Hill
University College, Ormskirk.

Front cover illustration: Guy at the Tournament
taken from *The History of Guy, Earl of Warwick*.
Derby: Printed by J Drewry, 1796.

GUY OF WARWICK
AND OTHER CHAPBOOK
ROMANCES

Six Tales from the Popular Literature of Pre-industrial England

edited by

JOHN SIMONS

UNIVERSITY
of
EXETER
PRESS

First published in 1998 by
University of Exeter Press
Reed Hall, Streatham Drive
Exeter, Devon EX4 4QR
UK

British Library Cataloguing in Publication Data
A catalogue record of this book is available
from the British Library

ISBN: 0 85989 445 2

Printed in Great Britain by Short Run Press Ltd, Exeter

Acknowledgements

I would like to thank the Huntington Library at which I held a Mayer Fellowship and the British Academy for providing the funding which enabled the bulk of the textual research to be carried out, and Edge Hill University College which provided a further small grant to support incidental production costs. Thanks are especially due to the staff of the Rare Books Room at the Huntington Library, who were unfailingly helpful and courteous during my stay there. Simon Townsend, Senior Museums Officer, Cherwell Area, kindly provided information on local historical studies of the Banbury chapbook industry. Dr Gillian Davies took the time to read the entire work in draft and to offer her insights. Julia Hedley gave valuable help and advice on the preparation of camera-ready copy. I have long-term debts of gratitude to Professor Maldwyn Mills, Professor Michael Swanton and Professor Chris Baldick, whose support and friendship have sustained me throughout my career.

Permission to reproduce illustrations of material in the Huntington Collection is gratefully acknowledged.

Introduction

Why Read Chapbooks?

This edition is designed to make available to the modern student good reading texts of chapbooks, the flimsy and often poorly printed booklets which were a major source of literature for the English poor in the eighteenth century and early nineteenth century.[1] There is a full discussion of the nature and form of chapbooks below as well as some analysis of their history and readership, but here I wish to set out some of the reasons for being interested in such apparently ephemeral objects and to comment on some aspects of the relationship between work on popular literature and culture and more mainline literary-historical studies.

Chapbook readers left few records of their tastes or opinions. They were, for the most part, in dire economic necessity and therefore did not have the leisure to record their thoughts, or else they were children and did not have the power.[2] To read chapbooks is, therefore, to enter a one-sided conversation with the past. We can listen to the chapbooks as they speak to their long-dead readers, but we cannot easily hear the readers speaking back. It is true that many people who were probably chapbook readers did leave autobiographical writings, but these tend to relate narratives of personal and political development. Only very rarely are details of aesthetic response recorded. Chapbooks thus force us into the reconstitution of the mentality of groups who left few relevant traces of themselves. When we read chapbooks we must constantly ask ourselves what pleasure they offered to a reader whose access to print was limited and what sense the picture of the world they offer would have made to him or her.

Such reconstructive studies are necessary if we are going to maintain any feeling for historical continuity. Only such a feeling will enable us to remember and understand the lives of people whose access to privileged forms of communication was limited or non-existent. They provide a salutary reminder that poverty of information is not necessarily a recent phenomenon and that it visits its ill effects on future generations just as surely as do years of bad nutrition. Such studies are also necessary if many contemporary students of English Literature are to be enabled to position themselves autobiographically in the continuum of their studies. A very large number of those who now work at all levels of the higher education system—as teachers, researchers or undergraduates—have personal and family histories which offer them little or no stake in the high culture which forms the core of their academic work. It is at least desirable that they should have some access to the artefacts which produced their ancestors' world-view rather than that of their ancestors' masters.

Chapbooks offer an exemplary body of texts for this purpose and they allow us to begin to grasp the textures of the world of the pre-industrial rural and urban poor as it appears through their common reading. Most people who begin to look at chapbooks seriously appear to find that they also offer some pleasures to the modern reader. These little paper objects were valued and loved by those who bought them both in childhood and maturity. Anyone handling them today cannot fail to be moved by the disjunction between their size and fragility and the status they appear to have held in the poor reader's mind. More than anything else it is this disjunction between monetary and affective value that speaks eloquently of the struggles of ordinary people to gain some pleasure and education from reading in a world which must, for most of them, have offered few opportunities for hope or self-realisation.

The Form and Cultural Contexts of Chapbooks

Before discussing in detail the chapbooks edited below, I will describe exactly what a chapbook is. There will then be a brief

OUTER

	Fold 2		Fold 3
Fold 4	4	5	12
Fold 1	21	20	13
Fold 4	24	17	16
	1	8	9

INNER

2	7	10
23	18	15
22	19	14
3	6	11

Figure: the make up of chapbooks. A single sheet of paper was folded into twelve to make a twenty-four page chapbook. The arrangement is that of the prose *Guy of Warwick* presented in this volume. The numbering of the pages before folding is shown; underlining indicates pages that will be printed upside down so that they are correct after folding. The sequence of folds is shown. Most chapbooks were sold in this folded form and the reader could then open and cut them to form a little pamphlet or, if she or he were wealthy, have them bound. Folding a sheet from a broadsheet newspaper according to the figure gives a very good sense of the physical reality of a chapbook.

the chapbook form—one can find chapbooks from Kendal, Whitehaven, Wigan, and Falkirk for example—but there were certain centres which gained and retained their prominence throughout the period. London, Newcastle, York, Glasgow (especially in the nineteenth century) and Banbury (represented by the work of John Cheney and the somewhat artistic productions of the Rusher family) were the most important of these.[12] A web of travelling pedlars known as chapmen spread from these regional centres where, particularly in London, printshops were supported by fully stocked warehouses. It was largely through this web that the chapbooks were carried all over the British Isles and reached the rural communities with which they are most commonly associated.[13] Thus the regions could be served with a range of chapbooks which not only linked them to national culture (for example, through chapbook texts of novels like *Robinson Crusoe* and *Moll Flanders*) but also satisfied local tastes (for example, the range of religious chapbooks produced at York or the highly colourful Scottish chapbooks of Dougal Graham, 'the bellman of Glasgow').[14] In this way, chapbooks provided one of the links which enabled national consciousness to grow within a culture which was still tolerant of regional difference. It has been very properly said that 'the importance of the printing press in unifying Great Britain and in shaping its inhabitants' view of themselves' has not been fully understood.[15]

Economic hardships made it unlikely that chapbooks would have formed a regular purchase in labouring households even in better times. However, we know from the autobiographical writings of such as John Clare, Samuel Bamford and Thomas Holcroft that chapbooks were a fairly familiar commodity among the rural poor.[16] It should be remembered that in pre-industrial societies (or in societies where industrialisation has not severely impacted on the details of daily life and culture) the lack of means to possess or read a text does not by any means preclude access to writing. Events where readings to village communities formed a common entertainment are well recorded for early modern France and Italy, and the bookseller James Lackington hinted at similar pastimes in eighteenth-century England when he wrote of:

> The poorer sort of farmers and even the poor country
> people in general, who before that spent their evenings
> in relating stories of witches, ghosts, hobgoblins etc.,
> now shorten the winter nights by hearing their sons and
> daughters read tales, romances etc.[17]

Even so, it is probably safest to assume that the regular purchase
and collection of chapbooks was available only to those members
of rural communities who lived in relative comfort (say on 10s a
week) and that these families played the part of culture brokers.
They mediated between the national life based in literacy and the
oral tradition which formed the fine texture of understanding and
belief in the mass of the population.[18] There are plainly many things
to be said against this simple model, but it is difficult to see how
the hard facts of economic life in pre-industrial England square
easily with any other interpretation. We should certainly not
assume that chapbooks were ephemera which could be read and
discarded. If only a smallish number has survived, this may well be
due to the process of 'reading to bits' and also the lack of affection
for these traditional texts which set in when the mass production of
genuinely cheap books and periodicals, often in penny and
twopenny issues, drove them from the urban market at least in the
1830s and 1840s.

We also know that, while the labourers read chapbooks in their
cottages, the children of the gentry also avidly consumed them in
the great houses. Through these children, the many servants who
laboured to support landowners, rural merchants and industrialists
may also have had access to them. Sir Richard Steele, James
Boswell, Sir Walter Scott and George Borrow all read chapbooks
as children, and in Boswell's case collected them in maturity.
Thackeray bought and enjoyed chapbooks on his tour of Ireland.[19]
One of the most intractable problems of chapbook scholarship is
that the best and most extensive bases of evidence for chapbook
readership comes not from the rural poor, who plainly did provide a
huge and diverse market for them, but from the gentry. This need
not disturb us too much if we remember that it was possible to be
able to read and to have access to chapbooks even if you were only

supported by a relatively low economic base and a restricted set of cultural opportunities. To have been able to write, however, especially to have been able to write with the kind of leisure that is implied by the ability to make records of personal literary taste, was an entirely different order of accomplishment. Put bluntly, it was a luxury which was even further beyond the reach of the English poor than the penny chapbook.

I remarked above that it is too often said that popular literature, and especially popular literature which has the low status ascribed to chapbooks, is designed to appeal to a reader of low sophistication and low intellect. Part of my purpose in producing this edition is to counter this highly prejudiced view. It is true that chapbooks do not speak to a world thronged by readers who were conversant with high literary culture or the finer points of literary discrimination. At the same time, the chapbooks themselves do not suggest a reader of low literacy. The texts presented here do not, to my mind, make concessions where literacy is concerned. They make the occasional blunder which may amuse a contemporary reader but which is understandable to anyone who can comprehend that a reasonable level of intelligence may readily combine with poor education.

Anyone who could read a *Moll Flanders* chapbook was certainly sufficiently literate to read *Moll Flanders*. What he or she may well not have been able to do was BUY *Moll Flanders* in any but its penny form. Chapbooks do not speak of a world of intellectual limitation but of a world of economic hardship and lack of opportunity. Working-class autobiography of the nineteenth century is a record of the consistently heroic effort to gain access to the products of the official literate culture. We should not be too quick to assume, especially when considering a world where hard work from childhood onwards left little room for education (even if this were an available option), that lack of money implies anything more than poverty and all the waste of human intellectual and sensual resources that poverty brings with it.

The Concerns of Chapbooks

Although chapbooks are most readily associated with highly traditional materials, this view does not do anything like justice to their range of interests. Indeed a chapbook collector could have assembled a library in miniature which comprehended almost the entire range of polite knowledge. In order to give some meaningful contexts to the chapbook romances edited below it will be helpful to review briefly the sorts of chapbook which their readers might also have owned and enjoyed.

Chapbooks were often of practical as well as recreational interest, so we may begin with mentioning the various almanacs and prognostications which were found in this form from the late seventeenth century onwards. Almanacs offered obvious guides to life in rural surroundings, but their purely practical uses were supplemented by more exotic books of prophecies. The most celebrated were probably those of *Mother Shipton* and *Mother Bunch*, with *Nixon's Cheshire Prophecies* coming a close third. These chapbooks blended folkloric material with obscure prophecy and biographies of the prophets.[20] It is hard to say how far such texts were used in a genuinely practical manner. They were certainly just the sort of work which gave chapbooks their bad reputation in the official culture where more reputable astrologers such as Partridge had long been the butt of fashionable jokes and had themselves passed into chapbook form. I suspect that many chapbook readers would have seen this kind of text as entertaining and absurd but containing much useful material and being of some historical interest.

More obviously practical were various guides to divination: the interpretation of dreams, the significance of the placement of moles on the face and body, physiognomy and palmistry. These sorts of popular sciences were the common currency of travelling fairs and would have been very familiar to rural readers who may have tried various sorts of divination for themselves—especially where the choice of a marriage partner was concerned. Indeed the key and Bible ceremony was a common popular practice (corresponding with the more polite *sortes Virgilianae*) and David Vincent has written an account of a *Guy of Warwick* chapbook being used in a divination ceremony where a Bible was lacking.[21] In addition to exploring the various supernatural forms of choosing a partner, chapbook readers could learn how to cement a relationship by reference to chapbooks which taught them how to write letters. This kind of chapbook, where a series of letters shows both the progress of a relationship and various other types of family situation, is particularly interesting for two reasons. The first is that such chapbooks do tend to have the force of miniature epistolary novels: the examples I have seen seem to lose sight of their practical purpose and become engrossed in the progress of the courtship which they are mapping. The second is that Samuel Richardson, the great exponent of the epistolary form in the mid-eighteenth century, served his apprenticeship with a chapbook printer and may have found his initial stimulation in his experience of producing chapbooks. It is probably no coincidence that Mr Colbrond, the tormentor of Richardson's heroine Pamela, shares his name with one of the major enemies of Guy of Warwick, a most durable chapbook hero whose adventures are edited in two versions below.[22] We see here just how dangerous it is to build watertight compartments between the different levels of cultural production, for just as it is certain that all late eighteenth-century adults are likely to have used opium for medicinal or recreational purposes at some point in their life, it is also certain that all polite adults are likely to have read chapbooks during their childhood and would have known very well the source of Richardson's villain.

Religious chapbooks were also common, though here we must exercise some care in distinguishing chapbooks from tracts. In the 1790s the Society for Promoting Christian Knowledge produced, through the work of Hannah More and others, tracts in forms which very precisely mimicked those of the chapbook.[23] Indeed, antiquarian booksellers who offer chapbooks for sale are frequently in possession of collections of these tracts rather than of chapbooks proper. This tractarian marketing ploy was so successful that there is the real probability that it forced chapbooks into a decline from which they never fully recovered (in the south of England at least). There were, however, also genuine chapbooks with a religious content. I have already mentioned the religious chapbooks which circulated in Yorkshire, but chapbooks which told biblical or quasi-biblical stories were well known and must have supplemented Bible reading and provided useful examples which could be easily recalled and discussed.

Related to religious chapbooks, especially to those of Hannah More, are the radical political tracts which were produced by Thomas Spence, also in the 1790s.[24] Spence was plainly-concerned with the issue of literacy and actually attempted the publication of a phonetic Bible to be sold in penny instalments. Thomas Paine's *The Rights of Man*, by far the most influential radical work of its time, also appeared in chapbook form.[25] By 1805 the publisher Thomas Harris had also begun to appropriate the forms of the children's chapbook in order to produce political satire.[26] The relationship between Blake's illuminated books, chapbooks and late eighteenth-century London radicalism should also be recognised and gives another important insight into the role which chapbooks had in mediating between different levels of cultural activity.[27]

One of the most difficult kinds of chapbook to place is that which contains a collection of songs. These collections are usually known as 'Garlands' and formed a very large part of the output of chapbook printers, particularly in London and Newcastle.[28] Frequently such texts do not run to the full twenty-four pages, but in all other respects they are true chapbooks in that they satisfy the formal criteria I outlined above. They are probably best seen as offering a parallel (and better value) form to the broadside ballads which are especially associated with the printers in the Seven Dials area of London and which would also have been available from chapmen.[29] Many Irish chapbooks, for example those printed by Walter Kelly of Waterford or William Gogarty of Limerick, are collections of songs in the Garland format.[30] Chapbook readers would certainly have been familiar with Garlands and probably bought them to supplement their collections, but the material contained in them is certainly different from that in other kinds of chapbook as it obeys formal conventions which are sometimes far removed from the traditional world of village culture.

Current affairs were frequently explored through broadside ballads, especially those which dealt with violent crime, accidents or the execution of notorious murderers. Chapbooks too reflected eighteenth-century society's obsession with crime. This obsession comprehended crime's potential as a subject both for exciting and romantic stories and for edifying narratives of penitence and punishment. The lives of pirates and famous highwaymen are represented in the chapbook stock and there are also chapbooks which provide awful warnings of the dangers of filial disobedience, avarice and inebriation—especially in combination. This kind of chapbook offered not only pious examples but also genuinely entertaining narratives, and must surely have been read as much for the enjoyment of prose fiction as for the guidance which they presented. Indeed this dual function can be readily recognised in the early eighteenth-century novel. Defoe plainly drew on the genre of Newgate biography for *Moll Flanders* and on sailors' memoirs for *Robinson Crusoe*, and it is no surprise to find that both of these texts were commonly produced in chapbook form. It is interesting to speculate, there being little formal difference between the biographies of genuine rogues and that of the fictional Moll Flanders, whether or not chapbook readers—who almost certainly would not have heard of Defoe—would have read these texts as pure fiction or whether they happily, or anxiously, assumed that they had a solid, if colourful, factual basis.

With rogue biographies we are approaching fiction proper and we may pass over chapbooks with a historical content and jest books (a hardy Tudor form which survived well into the eighteenth century through the chapbooks) and encounter fiction proper. I have already mentioned chapbooks of Defoe's novels, and there were also chapbook versions of work by Fielding. However, the core of chapbook fiction divides into three sections. The first contains romances, which form the subject of this edition and will be dealt with in detail below. The second consists of short self-contained anecdotes based on the life of a particular hero. The third is based on a range of traditional narrative. The second category usually has its sources in late medieval and Renaissance writing and concentrates on the lives of well-known figures such as

Faustus, Fortunatus, Dick Whittington (though Whittington chapbooks arguably belong to the genre of historical biography), Reynard the Fox, or Robin Hood. The third category contains some of the most interesting and charming narratives and is most frequently cited by readers who were remembering their childhood experience of chapbooks. In this category we find Jack the Giant Killer, Thomas Hickathrift and Tom Thumb. In these fascinating stories can be seen many strata of the history of English narrative. Elements drawn from Middle English romance jostle with apparently polite commentary and material which appears to derive from an oral tradition of story telling. We can usually assign definite early printed sources to parts of most of these texts, but there remains a residue that tantalisingly reminds us of the voices which once breathed through a now entirely dead culture.

It will be seen from the latter part of this very brief, highly descriptive and by no means exhaustive account of the range of chapbooks that, where fiction is concerned, it is extremely hard to draw a line which defines authoritatively where a text as record of historic fact ends and a text as record of imaginative creation begins. The lack of named authorship which is a feature of most chapbooks (the Scottish writers Dougal Graham and James Hogg are extremely rare examples of known chapbook authors) leaves the reader bereft of the usual markers which enable him or her confidently to place books into the various categories which make the modern mind feel comfortable. Such taxonomic anarchy is, to some extent, a general characteristic of pre-industrial literature, but it is magnified by chapbooks which teach us just how much highly literate readers depend on extra-textual prompting in the act of interpretation. The notion that we might fully be able to understand a text solely through the encounter with its words and its rhetorical and syntactic devices becomes even more of a critical chimera.

It is often said that the traditional nature of chapbooks supported a cultural conservatism which hindered the potential of the rural poor to offer a radical critique of the world in which they found themselves. This opinion is one that derives largely from comment on the French *bibliothèque bleue,* but it is possible to extrapolate from this range of scholarship in order to speak of chapbooks. The first thing to be said about this view is that there is no evidence whatsoever that the chapbooks enshrined any conscious ideological project to keep the poor in happy ignorance. If anything, polite thinkers worried that traditions of rural life prevented the country people from cultivating the attitudes which would enable efficient work and the disciplines necessary for industrial progress. Secondly, poverty and suffering are not things of which you remain ignorant as you are experiencing them, especially when examples of luxury and ease are daily visible. The history of rural England in the eighteenth and nineteenth centuries may be read as marked as much by popular protest of an often violent kind as by the peaceful continuation of the seasonal rituals of Merry England which were increasingly under attack by the twin forces of the Protestant settlement and the rationalism of the Enlightenment.[31] Thirdly, just because the forms and expression of a culture appear to have deeply traditional affiliations, that does not mean that the function of those expressions cannot be absolutely modern in its particular applications.

What this signifies is that pre-industrial people were not the slaves of their traditions any more than modern people are the slaves of their clothes. Tradition provides a vocabulary and a structure, but it provides rather than precludes ways of understanding the challenges of changing social conditions. Chapbooks do not offer a uniform world-view. Rather they show how readers who were cut off from access to the mainstream of learning were able to make some strides towards it. Chapbooks offered poor readers a range of literate experiences. However, we should not patronise them by assuming that they could not make sense of them in any but an uncritical way. We might also remember that the conservative world-view which is frequently associated with rural tradition may be, for the most part, a construct of modern scholarship.

Chapbooks and the Romance Tradition

Perhaps the most extraordinary feature of chapbooks is their preservation of texts whose history can be traced back to the

very narrative space from which pure chivalric adventure had been displaced.[37] But eighteenth-century villagers or early nineteenth-century craft workers found imaginative stimulation, contrast, and, perhaps above all, the precious sense that by reading such texts they were participating in the world of literacy and education to which they were only marginally connected. The history of working-class self-improvement in the later nineteenth century shows that this connection was an object of undoubted and hard-fought aspiration.

Guy of Warwick

This collection begins with editions of two different chapbook versions of *Guy of Warwick*. I make no apology for this apparent duplication as Guy of Warwick stands for the archetype of chapbook heroes. Indeed, *Guy* chapbooks are really the only kind to have received anything like extensive critical treatment, most notably in the work of R.S. Crane.[38] I do not propose here to duplicate the very full historical investigation of the *Guy of Warwick* narrative in all its manifestations which was carried out by Crane some eighty years ago. I want instead to provide the reader with some sense of the depths of the traditions which chapbook romances represent, and to show how chapbooks were far from careless abridgements of longer texts. Furthermore, the verse chapbook which is edited below is American in origin and this section will also pay some attention to the conditions which prevailed in the Colonial period and during the formative years of the United States as far as chapbooks were concerned.

Like the vast majority of Middle English romances, *Guy of Warwick* began its existence in an Anglo-Norman version probably composed in the first half of the thirteenth century. By the fourteenth century a number of different versions of the poem existed in English and these represent the two main forms of non-alliterative romance: couplet and tail-rhyme stanza. To give some idea of the scale of these poems, the couplet version in Cambridge University Library MS Ff. 2. 38, which was composed in the mid-fifteenth century, runs to some 11,976 lines. Versions of *Guy* appear in a number of other manuscripts and a version of a section of Guy's story was composed by John Lydgate in the mid-1420s, so it is not surprising to find *Guy of Warwick* among the earliest English printed books. Both Pynson and de Worde produced editions in *c.*1500. A very full version of the story (7,976 lines) was printed by Robert Copland in 1560 and this represents one of the very last printings of a Middle English romance for purely recreational purposes in anything like its original English form. As I suggest above, changes in taste and the increasingly unfamiliar language of medieval texts stimulated a gradual process of replacement by other forms of romance. At the same time, the social composition of their readership shifted and became increasingly less courtly in character as the sixteenth century progressed.

Guy of Warwick remained part of literary currency through ballads, most famously *A Plesante Songe of the Valiant Actes of Guy of Warwicke* which made the first of its many appearances in 1592 and told the story of Guy's adventures in truncated form.[39] In 1608 Samuel Rowlands, a writer of low-life, humorous and moral pamphlets, took up the challenge 'to revive the deeds of this dust-consumed Champion' in an abridged version written in somewhat dogged six-line stanzas.[40] In common with most of the later versions of the story of Guy, Rowlands treats the narrative as a basically repeated bipartite structure and does not include the third section which deals with the adventures of Guy's son Reinbrun. It is from Rowlands's version that chapbook texts of *Guy* most usually derive and these all exploit the strong contrast between Guy's secular life leading up to his marriage with Felice and his subsequent repudiation of earthly values. Again, there is a basically bipartite structure which balances Guy's prowess in tournaments with his adventures as a crusader and his retreat to a hermitage whence he emerges for his last heroic battle and deathbed reunion with his faithful wife.

Above all Guy is an English hero. His battles are not only to gain knightly reputation and to further the cause of Christendom: they are also designed to spread the name of England as a country of heroes and, eventually, to save the land from foreign invaders and other dangers. In this respect it is easy to see why Guy should have been an attractive figure to the publishers and readers of chapbooks. Guy offers a simple model of how English virtue can be depended on to triumph over the chicanery of a variety of foreigners. This is important as the circulation of chapbooks around the British Isles corresponds fairly exactly to the increasing growth of the sense of nationhood as a shared set of cultural and political values which, in some circumstances, might be deployed to build unity across fundamental social and regional difference. In the pre-industrial period there were no mass media nor any mass communication. Sharp economic distinctions and their consequent effect on educational opportunity and literacy meant that polite literature could not function as a reliable carrier of patriotic ideology. Chapbooks, however, permeated all strata of English society and a hero like Guy had an important role to play in the dissemination of ideas of Englishness even to those who, being without property, had no formal stake in the official political discourse of the day. This is not to say that any chapbook publisher had in mind that his productions might serve a specific ideological purpose: there is not a shred of evidence for this position (which has been put forward for the French *bibliothèque bleue*). Rather, *Guy of Warwick* chapbooks might be seen to take their place in wider cultural and political developments and provide some understanding of the ways in which the poor and underprivileged might have shared in the debates which formed English political life during the eighteenth century.[41]

A more immediate attraction of Guy is the foundation of his story in social distinction and the need to demonstrate that disadvantage of birth can be overcome by talent and merit. Guy's rejection by Felice is founded wholly in her sense of social superiority. His life as a knight errant in the first movement of the narrative is pragmatically directed towards the demonstration that someone of relatively humble social origins can perform superbly well in the aristocratic domain of chivalry. Medieval readers were used to this kind of narrative resolving itself in the revelation that the knight in question was, in fact, of princely birth, but Guy is not a hero of this kind: his ascent to an Earldom is fuelled by his ability to act out all the roles expected of a knight by means of natural ability, strength and talent, and not by accident of birth. The attractiveness of this line of argument to readers who themselves suffered constant disadvantage but who lived in a society where it was plainly possible to rise through merit and enormous struggle may readily be seen. It may also be noted, in contradiction to those who might be tempted to argue that chapbooks were deliberately designed to foster a conservative attitude and political docility, that the tractarian writer Sarah Trimmer saw many of the classic chapbooks as subversive. She was particularly horrified that they might 'encourage the young and uneducated to consider marriage outside their social sphere'.[42]

The first *Guy* chapbook edited below was printed by James Drewry of Derby in 1796. In form and content it matches fairly exactly the pattern of many other *Guy* chapbooks which were produced throughout the eighteenth century by numerous printers and which followed more or less closely, but often (as here) in slightly abridged form, the original *Guy of Warwick* chapbook text which was published in 1680 and is attributed to Samuel Smithson.[43] This in itself is interesting as it shows how once a chapbook text was established it could retain its form quite readily, presumably by being used as the copy-text for printers in other regional centres. The text edited here retains both the shape and the basic verbal content of other versions. This textual conservatism can be explained partly by the need of printers at the lower end of the publishing industry to maximise the efficiency of their operations and keep down costs by cutting out any originality in the process of chapbook production.

The nature of the readership might also explain this conservatism. We might reasonably assume that, in a milieu with few books, where the sense that literacy was not necessarily a universal accomplishment was strong and where some individuals gained access to chapbooks by having them read to them, the texts took on a solidity which was constantly reinforced by re-reading and re-hearing. In the absence of any great ability to pick and choose what you read or owned, it would have seemed important that a text entitled *Guy of Warwick* was nearly identical with another text of the same name which had been read or heard previously. We are all familiar with the phenomenon by which children who have well-known stories read to them are extremely sensitive to the slightest verbal changes and find them disturbing and highly unsatisfactory. I believe that the same was true of pre-industrial rural readers and that the verbal identity of one text with another was not only a guarantee of its legitimacy as a correct version but also an important element in the provision of aesthetic pleasure.

The huge task of abridging *Guy of Warwick* is carried out with tact and skill. The chapbook presents a narrative which hangs together convincingly and is able to contain the major episodes of Guy's life in a highly truncated form. The compiler of the original chapbook version did not attempt to fit every one of Guy's adventures into twenty-four pages. He or she made a careful selection of the main elements which form the story and thus was able to retain the emotional and moral force of the narrative and its clear bipartite structure without clouding it with non-essential detail or repetition. *Guy of Warwick* chapbooks operate at a consistently high level of moral tension and concentrate on the core experiences around which circulate the multifarious adventures of the longer versions. The heart of the narrative is exposed in these texts which are far from thoughtlessly or carelessly cut down. The durability and success of *Guy* chapbooks is surely to be accounted for as much through the skill of its original abridger as through any more prosaic explanation.

One element which Samuel Rowlands added to the Guy of Warwick story is the episode in which Guy goes into a graveyard and, picking up a skull, meditates on earthly vanity. The style and occasion of this incident comes straight from the Renaissance and shifts Guy very obviously into the mental world of the Stuart reader. The chapbook compiler has retained this incident and used it as a major element of the second half of the narrative where it stands in place of the more martial activities which, in the longer versions, provide a mirror image in the spiritual world of Guy's chivalric prowess in the secular. This is a good choice as repetition which works well over the long haul would become clumsy and tedious in the short space of the chapbook. When George Jerry Osborne of Newburyport, Rhode Island, came to print his version of *Guy of Warwick* in 1793, this incident became central to his highly compressed poetic account of the Guy narrative. Osborne's version, printed below, is based on Rowlands's 1608 poem but in all other ways it stands as an independent branch of the tradition of *Guy* chapbooks. The truncated account of Guy's early adventures which suggests that the reader may already have some knowledge of Guy's story gives way to a moral and philosophical meditation on the significance of life. The potential for such reflection is fully explicit in all versions of the *Guy* narrative but, by making it the subject of his chapbook, Osborne transforms Guy's story from moralised adventure to philosophical treatise. To understand why this might be we should spend some time considering the chapbook industry as it existed in North America.

In the late seventeenth century America imported most of its books and among the imports we not unnaturally find a good number of chapbooks. However, as the Colonies developed a more sophisticated cultural infrastructure and a printing industry which reduced literary dependence on the Old World, we do not see the growth of anything like the same scale of chapbook printing as that which existed in England and Scotland.[44] There are two main reasons for this. The first may be found in the generally higher literacy rates which obtained in the American Colonies and especially in New England. The second relates to the ways in which the British chapbook industry was founded on a richly interdependent relationship between producer and distributor. In America the chapman network did not operate in anything like the same way or in anything like the same social conditions, and this inhibited the growth of a similar chapbook-printing industry. Apart from imports or chapbooks directly copied from English originals, American chapbooks often seem to appeal to a different kind of reader. American chapbook producers like Chapman Whitcombe or Andrew Steuart address an audience which already seems to have distinctively American cultural interests. They use chapbooks to explore the phenomena of the New World in a language which, if not necessarily more sophisticated than that of the English chapbooks, appears to assume a higher level of general education than was to be found in England at the time.[45] This is not to paint a picture of a Colonial Arcadia peopled by highly educated and articulate citizens of the Age of Reason. Early American society had its servant class, many of whom laboured under conditions of indenture which gave them considerably less freedom than that enjoyed by their English counterparts. Similarly, the appeal of imported chapbooks testifies to enormous cultural continuities which the Atlantic passage had not yet disturbed. Nevertheless, chapbooks were not as widespread in North America as they were in Britain and it is very probable that this has as much to do with different levels of cultural expectation and opportunity as it does with the historical and geographical barriers to the creation of a chapbook industry in the style of the Old World.[46]

This sketch of the American scene puts Osborne's curious chapbook into a broadly comprehensible framework. As a European cultural token, *Guy of Warwick* is too well known and too powerful to be entirely removed from the stock of popular narrative. At the same time, there is no obvious aesthetic or commercial attraction in the reproduction of the established *Guy of Warwick* chapbook text, which had, in any case, been imported in fairly large numbers between 1680 and 1760.[47] Osborne therefore chooses to produce a chapbook which builds on the cultural expectation of readers who may well already own the traditional version: just as Rowlands converted Guy from Medieval knight into Renaissance courtier so Osborne converts him into Enlightenment philosopher. As might be expected in post-Revolutionary Rhode Island, Guy's Englishness is completely absent from Osborne's poem, which is preceded by an epigraph from the French—it would be difficult to imagine a more completely popularising gesture for the United States in the early 1790s.

Just as the conservative form of Drewry's chapbook seems totally adapted to the cultural environment of England, so Osborne's quirky poem works for the United States. What is fascinating is the ability of the same narrative to support such diverse and differently slanted versions. Chapbooks are productions which exist successfully only in as much as they satisfy very directly the demands of their audience. In America the demand for chapbooks was never as great as in England or Scotland, but Osborne shows how, even within this restricted market, both the chapbook and its traditional content were capable of adaptation to the new environment.

The Seven Champions of Christendom

If any reader were to search for proof that the canonised circle of English literary 'classics' does not represent what has actually been read or only represents the tastes of a relatively small section of the available reading public, then he or she need look no further than *The Seven Champions of Christendom*. This book made its first appearance in 1596 under the authorship of Richard Johnson, who wrote a second part in 1597.[48] Johnson's original enjoyed several reprints during the seventeenth century and John Kirke produced a dramatised version in 1634. *The Seven Champions* continued to be printed as an illustrated children's book into this century and a toy theatre version was still available in the 1970s.[49] It was also, arguably, a formative influence on the texts of the English Mummers' plays. Thus Johnson's text has been in print in some form or other for nearly four hundred years, not as an antiquarian curiosity or preserved in the amber of a scholarly edition from a university press, but as a living text designed to give enjoyment and instruction to a broad spectrum of readers. The chapbook here edited was printed in Shrewsbury in the 1730s and is based on Johnson's text.

Although Johnson published his work in the late sixteenth century, he drew on material that has a much deeper history. The central core of the adventures of St George, around which the other heroes' stories flow, is essentially a re-telling of the Middle English romance of *Sir Bevis of Hampton*. Sir Bevis, like Sir Guy of Warwick, is an archetypal English hero who began his career in an Anglo-Norman poem of the early thirteenth century. His story appeared in various Middle English verse forms (stanzaic and couplet) throughout the fourteenth and fifteenth centuries.[50]

Comparisons between Sir Bevis and St George have led to consideration of ancient Oriental story material, but Bevis had an international career and, from the thirteenth century onwards, this highly localised English hero pursued his somewhat thuggish adventures in Welsh, Irish, Italian, Norse, Dutch, Russian, Yiddish and, as late as 1881, Rumanian. Bevis, like Guy, also appeared in the list of the early English printers: de Worde (1500), Pynson (1503), Marsh (1558), Tisdale (1560), Copland (1565) and Alde (1568).[51] Johnson's decision to base his figure of St George on Bevis is thus remarkably similar to Rowlands's wish to revive the reputation of Guy of Warwick.

It is worth pausing for a while on Richard Johnson as a consideration of his literary works is an instructive exercise in the reconstruction of the historical process by which medieval romance was transmitted to the chapbooks. Johnson was a citizen writer in the fullest sense, as he was an apprentice and then a freeman of the City of London. He thus shared precisely the urban experiences and environment of his readership. During his career he tried his hand at a number of common Elizabethan and Jacobean genres—the Garland, the jest book, London history and topography, patriotic pamphlets, memorial verses, and rogue pamphlets—and did not scruple to plagiarise where it suited him.[52] Johnson also produced a romance and a parodic romance. His *Tom a Lincolne* (Part One, 1599; Part Two, 1607) was a collection of Arthurian motifs and other narrative material culled from the Middle English tradition, while *The History of Tom Thumbe* (1621) is a parody drawn from precisely the same material.[53]

Johnson's entire output is paradigmatic of the Elizabethan popular author, and what becomes very clear, not only from his romances but also from asides and references in his other works, is that he was deeply familiar with the Middle English romances. This familiarity would have been shared by other literate London citizens. We can, thus, see the first stage of the movement described above by which the courtly texts of the fourteenth century became the citizen texts of the sixteenth. We should not therefore be surprised to discover that *The Seven Champions of Christendom* contains not only a faithful account of the romance of

Sir Bevis, but much other material drawn from romances such as *Guy of Warwick* and *Chevelere Assigne* (probably known to Johnson from Copland's 1550 printing of *Helyas*). We should also not be surprised that *The Seven Champions* plainly struck a chord—if regular reprinting is accepted as a reliable indicator of popularity—with a wide audience.

From this start it is understandable that *The Seven Champions of Christendom* should have been an obvious choice for revision into chapbook format. If the tasks facing the *Guy of Warwick* compiler were huge in terms of compressing such a long poem into twenty-four pages, he or she at least had the advantage of a relatively clear narrative line which fell into two easily separable and fundamentally symmetrical blocks. *The Seven Champions* poses very different problems, though it too requires massive cuts to reduce it to an appropriate scale. In fact, the chapbook edited here only manages to fit the text into twenty-four pages by changing to a smaller typeface after page 19. Although the adventures of St George occupy the major part of Johnson's original work, they are intricately interlaced with the adventures of the other six champions: St David of Wales, St Anthony of Italy, St James of Spain, St Patrick of Ireland, St Dennis of France and St Andrew of Scotland. This means that the task of compiling a chapbook involves a considerable amount of control over the doings of these secondary heroes if the main narrative of St George is to retain its integrity and centrality to the plot as a whole. The chapbook just about achieves this but at the cost of some heavily truncated episodes which skate on the margins of intelligibility.

The chapbook comprises in a very short space a credible abridgement that reflects the complexities of Johnson's lengthy romance. The effect of the chapbook is that of a compilation rather than a linear narrative and this gives it an attractiveness in that it offers the reader a set of related stories which one could imagine being appreciated separately. Above all, though, the chapbook's concentration on the adventures of St George gives it an explicitly patriotic appeal and, as was the case with *Guy of Warwick*, we can place the circulation of this text within the developing discourse of nationhood. Whereas Guy stands alone as an exemplar of English heroism, St George demonstrates the superiority of the English when his prowess is compared with that of the heroes of the other major European nations. In addition, the mishaps that befall the other champions enable the reader to reflect on the iniquities of other foreign cultures.

The Seven Champions of Christendom also introduces a marvellous element into the world of chapbook romances. Giants and dragons are so commonplace as not to be classified within the realms of the abnormal, but here we also find a rich vein of magic and enchantment. Incidents such as the enchantments of Kalyb and Ormandine or the transformation of St Dennis into a tree are not uncommon in the corpus of Middle English romance, though their narrative function and significance is debatable. In the chapbook, magic serves to give variety to the heroes' adventures and also enables the narrative further to stress the power of St George as he is faced by and overcomes adversaries both natural and supernatural. We might also speculate that the magical element relates the text to the strata of folk tale, with which the rural readership at least would have been familiar. We can see, for example, in the reading and writing of John Bunyan—a man who might be seen as a typical chapbook reader, albeit one of unusual talent—a combination of knowledge of popular romance (almost certainly including *The Seven Champions*) and traditional tales which enrich each other in the formation of a personal religion.[54] Later readers like John Clare were also plainly involved in a cultural mediation between traditional oral material and popular romance drawn from the chapbooks. *The Seven Champions* not only brings to the audience a sample of literary culture but also offers a degree of reassurance to those who were primarily familiar with folk narrative.

This interplay is important when we try to place the chapbooks in the continuum of the cultural options which were probably available to eighteenth-century villagers. We can begin to see, for example, the growth of the clear distinctions between folk, popular and mass culture. Folk culture is specifically owned by the community which develops it and may have little or no meaning outside of that community. Popular culture consists of artefacts which may be 'bought in' but which are then adapted to very specific needs.[55] Mass culture, on the other hand, may be said to consist of artefacts presented unambiguously as commodities to be consumed and in which the community of readers has no real stake. In modern cultural studies one frequently encounters significant confusion between the three categories. However, eighteenth-century chapbooks can offer valuable insights into the formation of the modern cultural industry, and so into the cultural distinctions which are defined in the previous paragraph. *The Seven Champions* enables a rural reader who is 'schooled' in folk culture to adapt a text which appears from outside of his or her own needs and then to invest it with significance within a paradigm of understanding that has been formed by those needs. The longevity of chapbooks shows very clearly that their reception can be modelled as a continuous reformation of the same text within the changing demands of the community of readers. By the twentieth century, however, the very end of the chapbook tradition shows that the texts had finally been translated into the world of mass culture and the competition from more attractive and seemingly prestigious artefacts eventually guaranteed their extinction.

Parismus

Parismus is the earliest chapbook edited here. It dates from sometime between 1711, when its printer, Thomas Norris, moved his shop to The Looking Glass on London Bridge, and 1732. It therefore stands at the very beginning of the history of chapbooks proper. *Parismus* is a direct development from the increasingly cheap versions of popular texts produced by London printers such as Charles Tyas and Jane Bell (who also printed some of the earliest twenty-four page chapbooks) from the mid-seventeenth century onwards. Norris had set up shop at St Giles Without Cripplegate in 1695, so it is not impossible that the earliest versions of this chapbook were produced in the previous century.

Parismus, like *The Seven Champions*, is an abridgement of an Elizabethan romance: the original was produced by Emmanuel Forde in 1598 with a second part, *Parismenos*—also abridged

30

here—in 1599. The romances of Forde were an attempt to imitate for the English reader the complex cycles of chivalric narratives which derived from Spanish and, to a lesser extent, Portuguese originals. These began to enjoy a vogue in England from the 1580s onwards.[56] The fashion for these texts was stimulated by the enormous popularity of the romance of *Amadis de Gaulle* in France, and in England they were represented by three main cycles: that of Amadis, translated by Anthony Munday, that of Palmerin, also translated by Munday, and *The Mirror of Knighthood*, translated by Margaret Tyler, Robert Parry, and others.[57] Various writers, including Munday and Parry, produced free-standing imitations of this style of romance which supplemented these translated works. It is into this category of free-standing imitation that the works of Emmanuel Forde largely fall.

The so-called Peninsular romances are characterised by their enormous length, by complex interlacement of the adventures of numerous heroes, and by a tendency to replace the detailed description of combat which characterises many Middle English romances with a sentimental and moralised reflection on the significance of chivalric experience. In their earliest English forms it is probable that these romances appealed to a polite as well as a citizen audience. Sir Philip Sidney's *Arcadia*, for example, shows the very clear traces of the influence of this kind of text. It is, therefore, significant that its origin as a piece of coterie writing did not prevent this work from soon becoming one of the most frequently reprinted pieces of Elizabethan fiction. Forde seems always to have aimed his work at a citizen readership and *Parismus* was reprinted five times in the years up to 1640. Given the numerous references to these romances in contemporary sources and the number of editions which they went through, we may marvel that they are not as familiar to students of Elizabethan culture as the plays of Marlowe or Jonson.

The *Parismus* chapbook edited here is densely printed in a larger format than is common for chapbooks, though it still conforms to the standard twenty-four pages. Once again the compiler faced significant problems of abridgement which he or she overcomes with a marked degree of success. Considering the complexity of Forde's original text, I believe that the reader of this chapbook is presented with a coherent narrative which handles multiple adventures with a high degree of intelligibility. In addition the chapbook succeeds in varying the pace of the narrative so that description of adventures and combat are balanced by conversation and reflection on love and courtly behaviour. The reader of this chapbook will get a very good idea of the style and flavour of Forde's romance.

The style and content of *Parismus* provides a striking contrast with that of *Guy of Warwick* or *The Seven Champions of Christendom*. In the first place it is not based so directly in traditional material but derives solely from an authored work. This is by no means unusual for chapbooks but it does mean that the conditions under which the text might have been understood are subject to modification. The reader of *Parismus* is very directly tapping the mainstream of English literature, and has no wide latitude for placing the text within any pre-existing complex of traditional narrative or interpretative strategies. The pleasure of this chapbook was very precisely invested in the sense that the reader was participating in a literary culture which opened horizons beyond his or her immediate community. This could readily lead to a hypothesis that chapbooks themselves can be arranged hierarchically and that the chapbook audience itself was divided along lines which were defined by taste and sophistication.

We know already that the audience was divided—between those who could read for themselves and those who could not, between those who could afford to buy the texts for themselves and those who could not—and there is no obvious reason to doubt that there was a further division along lines of preference. At the same time we should remember that in rural communities at least the choice available to any individual was arbitrarily limited to the contents of the visiting chapman's pack, and that while it might have been possible to collect chapbooks which reflected specific tastes or preferences, such an enterprise would not have been easy. On the other hand it would be dangerous to assume that just because a chapbook with its origins in a text by Forde appears, to twentieth-century readers, to be superior to the anonymous *Guy of*

Warwick chapbooks, there is any reason to assume the same attribution of superior status by seventeenth-century or eighteenth-century readers. Modern readers frequently, indeed characteristically, use authorship as a guide to textual status, but while early modern readers may well have done the same thing, we have no real sense of their idea of the relative standing of many authors. In fact, chapbook readers may well have had no idea at all about the origins of their chapbooks or of the merits of different authors as they were seen by the London literati.

Furthermore, this text, which was printed at the very beginning of the period during which the production and distribution of chapbooks reached industrial proportions, might also be seen as appealing directly not to the rural and provincial audience who form the core readership for later examples but to the descendants of those citizens who had enjoyed the works of Forde at the beginning of the century. I am not suggesting that such texts did not enjoy a wider dispersal at this period, but that they may be said to look and read more like shortened versions of longer texts rather than savagely abridged chapbooks. The style of *Parismus*, for example, retains much of the ornate language of Forde and contrasts with the plainer English to be found in *Guy of Warwick* or *The Seven Champions of Christendom*. The romance writer Francis Kirkman, a good example of the kind of reader I have in mind, was, for example, reading *Parismus* as a schoolboy in 1673 and recorded the fantasies that the text stimulated in him just as the apprentices of the 1590s might have recorded their feelings about the works of Richard Johnson.[58] We see here some of the difficulties in being overly dogmatic about the composition of the chapbook reading public and how the best evidence for such readers consistently comes from individuals who, by virtue of their social position, were able to pass down their experiences in forms more permanent than those available to most English villagers.

Parismus is presented here as an example of an important group of chapbooks which have their sources in the second generation of romances. Chapbook readers of the eighteenth century appear not to have made the distinctions between medieval and post-medieval romance that is made by modern scholars. It is also the case that in more polite circles of the period there was some revival of interest in Elizabethan fiction. At much the same time, the first real medievalists were rediscovering Middle English romances and polite society more generally was becoming interested in medieval culture as a pattern for the Gothic sensibility.[59] This revival had little or no effect on the world of English villagers (except later when its final manifestations began to affect the material shape of the village environment as embodied in the parish church), but a text like *Parismus*—if it did indeed have a circulation outside London—shows how chapbook romances presented themselves to their readers simply as romances. We should also remember that, in the mechanisms by which popular culture is actually consumed, the presence of generic markers within a text count for far more than detailed distinctions of period or author. Such distinctions are the inventions of the literary historian or critic and are not necessarily important to the reader.

Valentine and Orson

The story of *Valentine and Orson* is usually identified as belonging to the genre of romance, but it has many elements which align it with folk-tale. Indeed, as an example of medieval romance it has a somewhat eccentric history, as the earliest English translation dates from c.1502 (very late) and the text is represented not by a manuscript but by early printed editions (by de Worde (1502) and, notably, by Copland (1550s)). The text clearly relates to the prose romances which were imported from France and Burgundy in the late fifteenth century. In these texts nuances of courtly behaviour and dialogue have begun to occupy narrative attention to a far greater extent than is the case for earlier narratives of chivalric adventure.[60] It is included here to demonstrate the ways in which chapbooks preserved almost the entire range of romance styles extant in the Middle Ages.

Versions of *Valentine and Orson* continued to be printed well into the seventeenth century and thus its appearance as a chapbook shows it following a historical trajectory which we have observed

INTRODUCTION

in the other texts edited below. The version edited here is a very good example of an early nineteenth-century London chapbook which conservatively reproduces the text as it had become established in the eighteenth century. As with *The Seven Champions of Christendom*, it is easy to see how a story which turns on transformation, magic and the myth of the wild man could easily have been drawn into a semi-oral culture in which the experience of chapbook reading and the memory of traditional story might mingle in the mind of the audience.

Valentine and Orson is a collection of many of the common motifs of European romance.[61] It represents the kind of composite production which marked the tailing off of the romance tradition in the later Middle Ages.[62] Episodes such as the false accusation of the Queen, the separation of twin brothers, and the tragic combat followed by pious retreat might in themselves form the building blocks of any number of texts, but here they are combined to make a satisfyingly coherent narrative. The reader who was experienced in the poetics of romance could easily find in *Valentine and Orson* the markers which would lead to an entry into the text and which would place the text within the mainstream of his or her literary experience. For example, anyone who had read or was familiar with *Guy of Warwick* chapbooks could find reinforcement of the themes of Guy's life as a crusader and his death as a hermit in the behaviour of Valentine at the end of the story. Similarly, the enchantment and transformation would have struck chords with readers who knew *The Seven Champions of Christendom*.

What I am trying to establish here is the sense that chapbooks exist in a rich intertextual matrix. Chapbook readers did not necessarily move from one text to another by applying a limited template of never-changing generic markers. Rather, the distillation of structure and motivic composition which is the characteristic feature of chapbooks is such that, in a highly conventional mode such as romance, textual differentiation is all but eroded away and we are left with highly concentrated narrative cores which retain the very essence of the original text. It might even be true to say that chapbooks are not so much abridgements as compressions of longer texts. The chapbook reader is faced with a corpus of

35

romance which appears as painfully limited to the modern eye but which actually offers up extremely powerful narratives which more than compensate for the lack of access to a wider choice of texts. In addition, the constant reinforcement of basic structure which chapbook romances provide may be necessary to fix generic markers in the minds of readers whose access to texts was hard won, arbitrary and often sporadic.

Valentine and Orson was a text which enjoyed a wide currency in Europe and had a marked effect on polite literature in England. However, whereas in France the *salon* fairy tales of the *précieuses* maintained a cultural continuity between the world of the *bibliothèque bleue* and the gentry, this continuity was extremely attenuated, if not actually absent, in England except in so far as the gentry themselves and, more particularly, their children were chapbook readers.[63] This possibly accounts for the fact that after the mid-seventeenth century the purest versions of *Valentine and Orson* are to be found in the chapbooks where its relationship with the folk tradition causes no social embarrassment.

The Seven Wise Masters of Rome

The Seven Wise Masters of Rome is not, strictly speaking, a romance. However, it is included here as it springs from the same narrative traditions as romance, may be closely associated with its concerns, and is frequently found in the same codicological environments (e.g. MSS Auchinleck, Cotton Galba E. ix., Cambridge University Library ff. 2. 38). Indeed, it has been suggested that the composer of the fourteenth-century version of *The Seven Sages* was also responsible for a number of romances.[64] Printed versions of this text appear very early (Pynson (1493), de Worde (1506), Copland (1555)). Production was continued into the seventeenth century when Purfoote released a version 'newlye corrected with a pleasaunt stile and purged from all old and rude words' (1602 and 1633). A Scots edition in verse by John Rolland was first printed in Edinburgh in 1578 and went through several editions up to 1635. From a bibliographical perspective, therefore, the history of this text is virtually identical to that of the true romances edited here and it shares its deep roots in ancient Oriental narrative with many medieval romances. There is also little doubt that the relatively late Middle English versions of this collection of stories were themselves influenced by the romances.[65] *The Seven Wise Masters* is a collection of short narratives which display proverbial wisdom and which provide the background for a highly conventional moral conflict between virtuous Prince and wicked Empress. The text was one of the most common chapbooks and its appeal is easy to understand in the light of the arguments about the nature of the relationship between chapbook readers and romance which were rehearsed above. The frame narrative permits a convincing degree of continuity and motivation from episode to episode. At the same time, the stories told by the Wise Masters and the counter-stories of the Empress in the struggle for the heart and mind of the Emperor and the life of the Prince are sufficient to stand alone as satisfying narratives in themselves. They thus offer the possibility of a good reading experience in a limited time.

This aspect of the chapbook very much reflects McSparran and Robertson's feelings about the medieval versions of the text:

> Its appeal in the fifteenth century, when Walter Paston, among others, owned a copy, probably reflects the variety of its stories, their bourgeois values and exemplary content.[66]

The proverbial wisdom of the Masters certainly fits well the more general world of the chapbook where readers were well accustomed to collections of wisdom literature, exemplary tales and also parodies such as *The Wise Men of Gotham*. The text is offered here not only as a final example of the ways in which chapbooks preserved the traditional forms of medieval romance but also as a way of linking this collection of a specialised sub-genre of chapbooks with the wider variety of texts available to the chapbook reader. The version edited here dates from 1817 and was produced by Thomas Johnston who was printing in Falkirk between 1798 and 1827. It is thus, appropriately for its position in this volume, an example of a fairly late chapbook and shows just how conservatively the chapbook printers operated in the preservation and transmission of their material.

This introduction has been an attempt to give the reader a short historical and critical contextualisation in preparation for his or her study of the texts which follow. The chapbooks have been selected to demonstrate the full range of styles of romance and together they show how the traditions of medieval narrative were made available to broadly based audiences in the eighteenth and nineteenth centuries. The volume is designed to provide a stimulation to further study both of the Middle English romances and of pre-industrial popular literature. It should also stimulate reflection on the nature of eighteenth-century literary culture in both its production and its reception and, more importantly, on the ways in which this culture is structured by modern scholarship. Above all, it is hoped that the experience of reading chapbooks will show that these humble productions have their own pleasures and deserve more than the relegation to footnotes, specialist bibliographical study, and broad generalisation that has most commonly been their lot in this century.

Notes on the Introduction

1. The only example of chapbook texts currently available is John Ashton's *Chapbooks of the Eighteenth Century* (London, 1882; repr. London, n.d. 1991?). This gives texts of some chapbooks but is largely of antiquarian rather than scholarly interest and consists mainly of plot summaries and reproductions of woodcuts. R.H. Cunningham, *Amusing Prose Chap-books* (London, 1889) gives fuller texts and V.E. Neuburg, *The Penny Histories* (London, 1968) contains seven facsimiles.

2. The issue of children as chapbook readers is by no means fully addressed in this volume but it is a vital area of chapbook research.

3. The best general treatments of the topic remain those of H.B. Weiss, *A Book about Chapbooks* (Trenton, 1942) and V.E. Neuburg, *A Chapbook Bibliography* (London, 1964). On America see H.B. Weiss, 'American Chapbooks 1722-1842', *Bulletin of the New York Public Library*, 49 (1945), pp. 491-8 and 587-98, W.L. Joyce et al. (eds), *Printing and Society in Early America* (Worcester, Mass., 1983), and V.E. Neuburg, 'Chapbooks in America', in C.N. Davidson (ed.), *Reading in America* (Baltimore, 1989).

4. See, for example, P. Burke, *Popular Culture in Early Modern Europe* (London, 1978), D.E. Farrell, 'The Origins of Russian Popular Prints and their Social Milieu in the Early Eighteenth Century', *Journal of Popular Culture*, 17 (1983), pp. 9-47, W.E.A. Axon, 'Some Twentieth-Century Italian Chapbooks', *The Library*, new series, 5 (1904), pp. 239-55, F.J. Norton and E.M. Wilson (eds), *Two Spanish Verse Chapbooks* (Cambridge, 1969), R. Darnton and D. Roche (eds), *Revolution in Print* (Berkeley, 1989), D.T. Pottinger, *The French Book Trade in the Ancien Regime* (Cambridge, Mass., 1958), R. Chartier, *The Cultural Uses of Print in Early Modern France* (Princeton, 1987), and R. Mandrou, *De La Culture Populaire au dix-huitième Siécle* (Paris, repr. 1985). R. W. Scribner, *For the Sake of*

Simple Folk (Oxford, 1994) is a valuable study of popular literacy during the German Reformation.

5. See G. Armistead and J. Silvermann (eds), *The Judaeo-Spanish Chapbooks of Yacob Abraham Yona* (Berkeley, 1971). On *folhetos* see P. Burke, 'Chivalry in the New World', in S. Anglo (ed.), *Chivalry in the Renaissance* (Woodbridge, 1990), pp. 252-62, and W. Rowe and V. Schelling, *Memory and Modernity* (London, 1991), pp. 85-94. On Nigerian chapbooks see B. Lindfors, 'Heroes and Hero-Worship in Nigerian Chapbooks', *Journal of Popular Culture*, 1 (1967), pp. 1-22, and E.N. Obiechina, *Onitsha Market Literature* (London, 1972).

6. A few scholars have recently looked at the wider implications of popular reading. See M. Spufford, *Small Books and Pleasant Histories* (Cambridge, 1981), a fascinating and invaluable study based on Samuel Pepys's collection of chapbooks and other popular texts. See also D. Vincent, *Literacy and Popular Culture 1750-1914*, (Cambridge, 1989), T. Watt, *Cheap Print and Popular Piety 1550-1640* (Cambridge, 1991), J. Friedman, *Miracles and the Pulp Press during the English Revolution* (London, 1993), P. Anderson, *The Printed Image and the Transformation of Popular Culture 1790-1860* (Oxford, 1991) and B.E. Maidment, *Reading Popular Prints, 1790-1870* (Manchester, 1996).

7. For a discussion of the transmission of polite literature into chapbook form see P. Rogers, *Literature and Popular Culture in Eighteenth-Century England* (Brighton, 1985) and 'Classics and Chapbooks', in I. Rivers (ed.), *Books and their Readers in Eighteenth-Century England* (Leicester, 1982), pp. 27-46. On serial publication see E.W. Pitcher, 'The Serial Publication and Collecting of Pamphlets, 1790-1815', *The Library*, 5th series, 30 (1975), pp. 322-9. J.P. Hunter, *Before Novels* (London, 1990) gives a good account of studies in the growth of literacy 1600-1800 on pp. 61-85. Hunter suggests that by 1800 60-70 per cent of adult men in England and Wales were literate with a rate of 88 per cent for Scotland. Female literacy was probably between 40-50 per cent. Literacy was higher in towns than in the country and highest in London, the south-east and the north. In 1832 *The Penny Magazine* first appeared and the preface to the first volume estimated a sale of two hundred thousand copies and a million readers.

8. Rule, *The Labouring Classes in Early Industrial England, 1750-1850* (London, 1986), pp. ix-x.

9. See Vincent, *Literacy and Popular Culture* and *Bread, Knowledge and Freedom*.

10. See D. Vincent, 'The Decline of the Oral Tradition in Popular Culture' in R.D. Storch (ed.), *Popular Culture and Custom in Nineteenth-Century England* (London, 1982), pp. 20-47, and D. Harker, *Fakesong* (Milton Keynes, 1985), pp. 40-41.
11. See P. Stockham, *Chapbooks* (London, 1976) and A.R. Thompson, 'Chapbook Printers', *Bibliotheck*, 6 (1972), pp. 76-83.
12. See, for example, V.E. Neuburg, 'The Diceys and the Chapbook Trade', *The Library*, 5th series, 24 (1969), pp. 219-31, F.M. Thompson, *Newcastle Chapbooks* (Newcastle, 1969), P.G. Isaac, *Halfpenny Chapbooks by William Davison* (Newcastle, 1971), S. Roscoe and A. Brimmel, *James Lumsden and Son of Glasgow* (London, 1981), F.W. Ratcliffe, 'Chapbooks with Scottish Imprints in the Robert White Collection', *Bibliotheck*, 4 (1964), pp. 88-174, E. Pearson, *Banbury Chapbooks* (Welwyn Garden City, 1970), P. Renold, 'William Rusher: A Sketch of his Life', *Cake and Cockhorse*, 11 (1991), pp. 218-28, P. Ward, *Cambridge Street Literature* (Cambridge, 1978), pp. 33-9.
13. The most detailed study of chapmen is M. Spufford, *The Great Reclothing of Rural England* (London, 1984). See also R. Leitch, 'Here chapman billies tak their stand', *Proceedings of the Society of Antiquarians of Scotland*, 128 (1990), pp. 173-88 and P. Rogers, 'Defoe's *Tour* (1742) and the Chapbook Trade', *The Library*, 6th series, 6 (1984), pp. 275-9.
14. See Rogers, 'Classics and Chapbooks', C.A. Federer, *Yorkshire Chapbooks* (London, 1899), G. MacGregor (ed.), *The Collected Writings of Dougal Graham*, 2 vols (Glasgow, 1883), W. Harvey, *Scottish Chapbook Literature* (Dundee, 1903).
15. Colley, *Britons* (London, 1992), p. 40. See also R.A. Houston, *Scottish Literacy and the National Identity* (Cambridge, 1985).
16. John Clare, *Autobiographical Fragments*, ed. E. Robinson (Oxford, 1986), pp. 56-7, Samuel Bamford, *Early Days* (London, 1849), Thomas Holcroft, *Hugh Trevor*, ed. S. Deanes (Oxford, 1973), p. 41. See also G. Deacon, *John Clare and the Folk Tradition* (London, 1983).
17. Cited by R. Porter, *English Society in the Eighteenth Century* (Harmondsworth, 1982), p. 253. E.P. Thompson, *The Making of the English Working Class* (Harmondsworth, 1963) records cases of labourers reading to their colleagues. See also D. Worrall, *Radical Culture* (London, 1992).
18. Burke, 'The "Discovery" of Popular Culture', in R. Samuel (ed.), *People's History and Socialist Theory* (London, 1981), pp. 216-21.

Louis James, *Fiction for the Working Man* (London, 1963) argues convincingly for the formation of a new urban literate culture which 'was not a continuation of the old popular cultures which expressed themselves in broadsheets, chapbooks and popular drama' (p. 1). From the 1820s onwards this new culture, specifically urban in character, was provided with a host of cheap books and periodicals such as *The Penny Magazine* (see note 7 above). These new publications covered much of the same ground as chapbooks but often with a more explicitly educational purpose. However, even *The Penny Magazine* drew attention to the fact that 'some of the unexampled success of this little work is to be ascribed to the liberal employment of illustrations, by means of Wood-cuts' (Preface to issue 1).

19. See, for example, R. Steele, *The Tatler*, no. 95, J. Boswell, *Boswell's London Journal*, ed. W.A. Pottle (London, 1950), p. 299, George Borrow, *Lavengro* (Oxford, 1982), p. 67, J.C. Corson, 'Scott's Boyhood Collection of Chapbooks', *Bibliotheck*, 3 (1962), pp. 202-18, W.M. Thackeray, *The Irish Sketch Book*, 2 vols (London, 1843), I, p. 7 and II, pp. 273-4.
20. Ashton, *Chapbooks of the Eighteenth Century*, gives examples of these. See also D. Valenze, 'Prophecy and Popular Literature in the Eighteenth Century', *Journal of Ecclesiastical History*, 29 (1978), pp. 75-92 and B. Capp, *Astrology and the Popular Press* (London, 1979).
21. Vincent, *Literacy and Popular Culture*, p. 177.
22. Simons, 'Romance in the Eighteenth-Century Chapbook' in J Simons (ed.), *From Medieval to Medievalism* (London, 1992), pp. 122-43, p. 130.
23. See V.E. Neuburg, *Popular Literature* (Harmondsworth, 1977), pp. 249-64.
24. On Spence see M. Wood, *Radical Satire and Print Culture* (Oxford, 1994), pp. 86-95.
25. Ibid., p. 94
26. Ibid., pp. 222-5
27. On Blake and chapbooks see G. Summerfield, *Fantasy and Reason: Children's Literature in the Eighteenth Century* (London, 1983) and P. Ackroyd, *Blake* (London, 1995), pp. 24-5.
28. See Thompson, *Newcastle Chapbooks*.
29. For surveys of these genres and many examples see C. Hindley, *Curiosities of Street Literature* (Welwyn Garden City, 1969), L. Shepard, *The History of Street Literature* (Newton Abott, 1973), L. James, *Print and the People* (Harmondsworth, 1978), L. Shepard, *The*

NOTES ON THE INTRODUCTION

Broadside Ballad (Wakefield, 1978), C.M. Simpson, *The British Broadside Ballad and its Music* (New Brunswick, 1986).

30. On these printers see J. Simons, 'Irish Chapbooks in the Huntington Library', *Huntington Library Quarterly*, 57 (1995), pp. 359-65
31. See D. Cressy, *Bonfires and Bells* (London, 1989), E.P. Thompson, *Customs in Common* (Harmondsworth, 1991), R. Hutton, *The Rise and Fall of Merry England: The Ritual Year 1400-1700* (Oxford, 1994), Hunter, *Before Novels*, pp. 138-64. Hunter points out (p. 147) that John Locke was so traumatised by the folk stories told him by his childhood nurse that he was scared of the dark and the hobgoblins that lurked there throughout his life.
32. The most recent general survey is that of W.R.J. Barron, *English Medieval Romance* (London, 1987).
33. See G. Doutrepont, *Les Mises en Prose des Epopées et Romans Chevaleresques* (Brussels, 1939), N.F. Blake, 'William Caxton's Chivalric Romances and the Burgundian Renaissance in England', *Essays and Studies*, 57 (1976), pp 1-10, and N.F. Blake, 'Lord Berners: A Survey', *Medievalia et Humanistica*, 2 (1971), pp. 119-32.
34. Simons, 'Medieval Chivalric Romance and Elizabethan Popular Literature' (Exeter University unpubl. Ph.D., 1982).
35. See F. Braudel, *The Mediterranean in the Age of Philip II*, 2 vols (London, 1975).
36. Mish, 'Black Letter as a Social Discriminant', *Publications of the Modern Language Association of America*, 68 (1953), pp. 627-30.
37. See J. Simons, 'Open and Closed Books: a Semiotic Approach to the History of Elizabethan and Jacobean Popular Romance', in C. Bloom (ed.), *Jacobean Poetry and Prose* (London, 1988), pp. 8-24 and J. Simons, 'Transforming the Romance: Some Observations on Early Modern Popular Narrative', in W. Gortschacher and H. Klein (eds), *Narrative Strategies in Early English Fiction* (Lewiston, 1995), pp. 273-88.
38. Crane, 'The Vogue of Guy of Warwick from the Middle Ages to the Romantic Revival', *Publications of the Modern Language Association of America*, 30 (1915), pp. 125-94.
39. A version of this song was printed in Bishop Percy's *Reliques of Ancient English Poetry* (London, 1765).
40. Rowlands's works have been edited by E. Gosse, *The Works of Samuel Rowlands* (Glasgow, 1880).
41. See Simons, 'Romances in the Eighteenth-Century Chapbook', pp. 131-2.

42. Wood, *Radical Satire*, p. 221. The point is reinforced by A. Richardson, *Literature, Education and Romanticism* (Cambridge, 1994), who describes the Tractarian project (including Trimmer's own *Family Magazine*) as being part of 'a "popular" literature devised by the dominant groups to serve their own purposes' (p. 31). P. Joyce touches on similar issues in nineteenth-century chapbooks in *Democratic Subjects* (Cambridge, 1994), pp. 188-90.
43. See Crane, 'The Vogue of Guy of Warwick', pp. 171-4.
44. See J.D. Hart, *The Popular Book* (Berkeley, 1961), E. Wolf II, *The Book Culture of a Colonial American City* (Oxford, 1988), p. 69, M. Kiefer, *American Children through their Books* (Philadelphia, 1948), p. 10, R. Nye, *The Unembarrassed Muse* (New York, 1970), p. 23.
45. See V.E. Neuburg, 'Chapbooks in America', in Davidson (ed.), *Reading in America*.
46. See F.L. Schick, *The Paperbound Book in America* (New York, 1958), p. 42, L. Leary, *The Book-Peddling Parson* (Chapel Hill, 1984), D. Jaffee, 'Peddlers of Progress and the Transformation of the Rural North 1760-1860', *Journal of American History* (1991), pp. 511-35, W.J. Gilmore, *Reading Becomes a Necessity of Life* (Knoxville, 1989), R. D. Brown, *Knowledge is Power* (Oxford, 1989).
47. See Hart, *The Popular Book*, pp.15-7.
48. On Johnson see H.W. Wilkomm, *Uber Richard Johnson's Seaven Champions of Christendome* (Berlin, 1911), J. Simons, 'Medievalism as Cultural Process in Pre-industrial Popular Literature', *Studies in Medievalism*, 7 (1995), pp. 5-21.
49. Pollock's Toy Theatre: *The Seven Champions of Christendom* (London, 1972).
50. For an account of the various texts of Bevis with a supporting bibliography see J.B. Severs, *A Manual of the Writings in Middle English*, I (New Haven, 1967), pp. 25-7.
51. There is a full account of the printing history of *Bevis* in J. Fellows, '*Bevis Redivivus*: The Printed Editions of *Sir Bevis of Hampton*', in J. Fellows, R. Field, G. Rogers and J. Weiss (eds), *Romance Reading on the Book* (Cardiff, 1996), pp. 251-68.
52. See F.B. Williams Jr., 'Richard Johnson's Borrowed Tears', *Studies in Philology*, 34 (1937), pp. 186-90 and R.S.M. Hirsch, 'The Source of Richard Johnson's *Look on Me London*', *English Language Notes*, 13 (1975), pp. 107-13.
53. These texts have both had modern editions: R.S.M. Hirsch, *The Most Pleasant History of Tom a Lincolne* (New York, 1978), C.F. Buhler, *The History of Tom Thumbe* (Evanston, 1965).

54. Salzman, *English Prose Fiction 1558-1700* (Oxford, 1985), p. 244.
55. Burke, *Popular Culture in Early Modern Europe*, p. 60.
56. See H. Thomas, *Spanish and Portuguese Romances of Chivalry* (Cambridge, 1920).
57. See D. O'Connor, *Amadis de Gaulle* (New Brunswick, 1970), G.R. Hayes, 'Anthony Munday's Romances of Chivalry', *The Library*, 4th. series, 6 (1925), pp. 57-81, M. Patchell, *The Palmerin Romances* (New York, 1947) and J. Simons, 'Robert Parry's *Moderatus*: A Study in Elizabethan Romance', in Fellows et al. (eds), *Romance Reading*, pp. 237-50.
58. Wright, *Middle-Class Culture in Elizabethan England* (Chapel Hill, 1935), pp. 86-7.
59. Wasserman, *Elizabethan Poetry in the Eighteenth Century* (Urbana, 1948), pp. 253-9.
60. See note 32 above.
61. Dickson, *Valentine and Orson: A Study in Late Medieval Romance* (New York, 1929) is an exhaustive survey of this text and its analogues.
62. Barron, *Medieval English Romance*, p. 195.
63. See J. Zipes, *Beauties, Beasts and Enchantments* (New York, 1991), D.R. Thelander, 'Mother Goose and her Goslings: The France of Louis XIV as Seen Through the Fairy Tale', *Journal of Modern History*, 54 (1982), pp. 467-96. J. Ladurie, *Love, Death and Money in the Pays d'Oc* (Harmondsworth, 1984) is a study of the interfaces between polite and popular culture in nineteenth-century Provence.
64. Pearsall (ed.), *The Auchinleck Manuscript* (London, 1979), p. xi.
65. Hibbard, *Medieval Romance in England* (New York, 1924), pp. 174-83.
66. McSparran and P.R. Robinson (eds), *Cambridge University Library MS Ff. 2. 38* (London, 1979), p. x.

Commentary on the Illustrations

Most chapbooks are illustrated with one or more woodcuts or, particularly with later texts, wood engravings. Sometimes printers had sets of blocks which related to specific texts and used them appropriately, but they also had collections of generic illustrations which crop up time and again in titles which often bear little relation to the cut. For example, I have seen a cut of the Emperor Nero used, for no apparent reason, to illustrate a *Moll Flanders* chapbook. Variants of the same cut, showing identical compositional features but differing in detail, can be traced from printer to printer (see illustrations 3 and 17 or the caption to illustration 1).

There can be little doubt that the illustrations were one of the features that attracted readers to chapbooks. Plainly, the pictorial commentary on the text which the more discriminating printers used woodcuts to provide enables some access to the narrative by even the most profoundly illiterate member of the audience. The woodcuts also help to give a clue to the content of the book and act almost as a trade-mark to certain texts. This may have helped readers to make their choices and chapmen to advertise their wares. Readers may also have been familiar with single sheet engravings such as those issued by the firm of Bowles and Carver in the 1780s and 1790s. Some of these prints illustrate chapbook subjects such as the life of Dick Whittington or the Wise Men of Gotham and such sheets must have supplemented the diet of print culture available to the chapbook audience, although their style is, generally, more sophisticated than that found in the chapbook cuts.

The illustrations in this volume show all the cuts in three of the chapbooks here edited. They give a good idea of the different styles which printers might adopt, from the more or less consistent use of tailor-made cuts by Norris to the exploitation of stock items sometimes only dubiously related to the text in hand (see illustration 15).

Editorial Note

This edition is not designed as a near facsimile nor as a guide to the typographical peculiarities of the texts. Original paragraphing, punctuation and spelling are retained but capitalisation and italicisation follow modern conventions. Misprints have not been corrected but are only recorded in the notes if they are of special interest. Errors which appear to be the result of misunderstanding on the printer's part have also been retained as offering insight into the mental world of the reader and are noted where appropriate.

Guy of Warwick
(Prose)

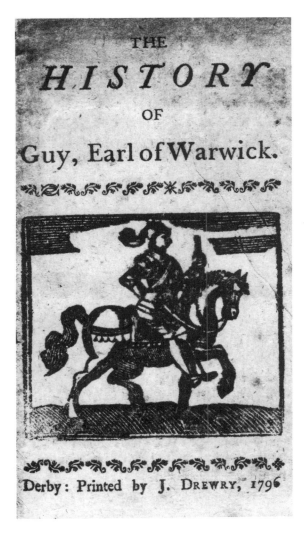

THE
HISTORY
OF
Guy, Earl of Warwick.

Derby : Printed by J. DREWRY, 1796

1.   The Title Page of *Guy of Warwick*.

This shows the printing details and a cut of a knight. It is a slightly simplified version of the cut which is commonly found on the title-pages of *Guy* chapbooks. This shows a knight in substantially the same attitude but he is accompanied by a lion and has a boar's head stuck on the end of his lance. See Ashton's *Chapbooks of the Eighteenth Century*, p. 140 and p. 154 for two variants (London and Newcastle) of the more common version.

THE

HISTORY

OF

Guy, Earl of Warwick[1]

Derby: Printed by J. Drewry, 1796

The History of Guy, Earl of Warwick

CHAPTER I

Guy's Praise. He falls in Love with Fair Phillis

In the blessed time when Athelstone wore the crown of the English nation, Sir Guy (Warwick's mirror and the world's wonder) was the chief hero of the age; whose process[2] so surpassed all his predecessors, that the trump of fame so loudly sounded Warwick's praise, that Jews, Turks and Infidels became acquainted with his name.[3]

But as Mars, the God of Battles was inspired with the beauty of Venus, so our Guy, by no man conquered was conquered by love; for Phillis the fair, whose beauty and whose virtue were inestimable shining with such heavenly lustre, that Guy's poor heart was ravished in adoration of his heavenly Phillis, whose beauty was so excellent, that Helen the pride of all Greece, might seem as a black a moor to her.

Guy resolving not to stand doating at a distance, went to Warick castle, where Phillis dwelt, being daughter and heiress to the Earl of Warwick; the Earl her father hearing of Guy's coming, entertained him with great joy; after some time the Earl invited Guy to go hunting with him; but he finding himself unable to partake of the diversion, feigning himself sick, the Earl troubled for his friend Guy, sent his own physician to him. - The doctor told Guy his disease was dangerous, and without letting blood there was no remedy. - Guy replyed, I know my body to be distempered, but you want skill to cure the inward inflammation of my heart;

Galen's[4] herbal cannot quote the flower I like for my remedy I know my own disease, doctor, and am obliged to you.

The doctor departed, and left Guy to cast his eyes on the heavenly face of his Phillis, as she was walking in a garden full of roses and other flowers.

CHAPTER II

Guy courts fair Phillis, she at first denies, but afterwards grants his suit, on Conditions which he accepts

Guy immediately advanced, to fair Phillis, who was reposing herself in an harbour[5], and saluted her with bended knees. All hail, fair Phillis, flower of beauty, and jewel of virtue, I know great princes seek to win thy love, whose exquisite perfection might grace the mightiest monarch in the world: yet may they come short of Guy's real affection; in whom love is pictured with naked truth and honesty, disdain me not for being a steward's son, one of thy father's servants. Phillis interrupted him, saying, Cease bold youth, leave off this passionate address. - You are but young and meanly born and unfit for my degree; I would not my father should know this passion

Guy, thus discomfited, lived like one distracted, wringing his hands, resolving to travel through the world to gain the love of Phillis; or death to end his misery. Long may dame Fortune frown, but when her course is run she sends a smile to cure the hearts that have been wounded by her frowns so Cupid sent a powerful dart, representing to her a worthy knight of chivalry, saying, This knight shall become so famous in the world, that his actions shall crown everlasting posterity. When Phillis found herself wounded she cried, O pity me, gentle Cupid, solicit for me to thy mother, and I will offer myself up at thy shrine.

Guy, little dreaming of this so sudden thaw, and wanting the blame[6] of love to be applied to his sores, resolves to make a second encounter. - So coming again to his Phillis, said, Fair Lady, I have

2.   Guy's courtship of Phillis.

Note how the lovers are figured in what appears to be Georgian costume. This kind of anachronism is very common in chapbook illustration.

been arraigned long ago, and now am come to receive my just sentence from the tribunal of love: It is life or death, fair Phillis, I look for; - let me not languish in despair, give judgement, O fair, give judgement, that I may know my doom, a word from thy sacred lips can cure my bleeding heart, or a frown can doom me to the pit of misery. - Gentle Guy, said she, I am not at my own disposal, you know my fathers name is great in the nation, and I dare not match without his consent.

Sweet lady, said Guy, I make no doubt but quickly to obtain his love and favour, let me have thy love first, fair Phillis, and there is no fear of thy father's wrath preventing us - It is an old saying, get the good-will of the daughter, and that of the parent will follow.

Sir Guy, quoth Phillis, make thy bold atchievements and noble actions shine abroad, glorious as the sun, that all opposers may tremble at thy high applauded name, and then thy suit cannot be denied.

Fair Phillis, said Guy, I ask no more - Never did the hound mind more his game, than I do this my new enterprize. Phillis, take thy farewell, and accept of this kiss as a signet from my heart.

CHAPTER III

Guy wins the Emperor's Daughter from several Princes. He is set upon by sixteen Assassins, whom he overcomes.

Thus noble Guy at last disengaged from love's cruelty, he now arms himself like a knight of chivalry, and crossing the ranging[7] ocean, he quickly arrived at the court of Thrace, where he heard that the Emperor of Almain's fair daughter Blanch, was to make a prize for him that won her in the field; upon which account the worthies of the world assembled to try their fortunes. - The golden trumpets sounded with great joy and triumph, and the stately pampered steeds prance over the ground, and each thought himself a Caesar, that none could equal; kings and princes being there, to behold who should be the conqueror, every one thinking that fair Blanch should be his.

3.   Guy at a tournament.

4.   Guy in the emperor's presence.

After desperate charging with horse and man, much blood was shed, and prince no more valued than vulgar persons[8]; but our noble Guy appearing, laid about him like a lion, among the princes; here lay one headless, another without a leg or an arm, and there a horse - Guy still like Hercules, charged desperately, and killed a German prince, and his horse under him. Duke Otto vowing revenge upon our English champion, gave Guy a fresh assault, but his courage was soon cooled. Then Duke Poyner would engage our favorite knight[9]; but with as little success as the rest, so that no man could encounter Guy any more; by which valour he won he lady in the field as a prince, being the approved conqueror The emperor himself being a spectator, he sent a messenger for our English knight - Guy immediately came into the emperor's presence, and made his obeysance; when the emperor as a token of affection, gave him his hand to kiss, and withal resigned him his daughter, and falcon and the hound. - Guy thanked his majesty for this gracious favour, but for fair Phillis's sake, left fair Blanch to her father's tuition, and departed from that graceful court, only with the other tokens of victory.

Now Guy beginning to mediate[10] upon his long absence from his fair Phillis and doubting of her prosperity; or that she might too much forget him, because the proverb says, out of sight, out of mind; prepared for England, and at last arrived at the long-wish'd for haven of his love; and with this sort of salutation greeted his beloved mistress; Fair foe, said he, I am now come to challenge your promse, the which was, upon my making my name famous by martial deed, I should be the master of my beloved mistress. - Behold, fair Phillis, part of the prize which I have won in the field, before kings and princes.

Worthy knight, quoth Phillis, I have heard of thy winning the Lady Blanch from royal dukes and princes, and I am glad to find that Guy is so victorious - But indeed Guy thou must seek more adventures.

Guy, discomfited at this answer, taking leave of his fair Phillis, clad himself again in Bellona's livery and travelled towards Sedgwin, Duke of Novain, against whom the Emperor of Almain had then laid siege. - But as Guy was going his intended journey,

Duke Otto, whom Guy had disgraced in battle, hired sixteen base traitors to slay him. Guy being set upon by these rogues, drew his sword, and fought till he had slain them all; and leaving their carcases to the fowls of the air, he pursued his journey to Louvain, which he found closely besieged, and little resistance could the duke make against the emperor's power. - Guy caused the Levinians to fall forth and made most bloody slaughter amongst the Almains; but the emperor gathering more forces, renewed the siege, thinking to starve them out; but Guy in another sally defeated the Almains, slaying in these two battles about thirty thousand men. - After this Guy made a perfect league between the emperor and the duke, gaining more praise thereby than by his former victories.

CHAPTER IV

Guy having performed great Wonders Abroad, returns to England, and is married to Phillis

After a tedious journey Guy sat down by a spring to refresh himself and he soon heard a hedious noise and presently espied a lion and a dragon fighting and tearing each other, but Guy perceiving the lion ready to faint, encountered the dragon, and soon brought the ugly Cerberes roaring and yelling to the ground - The lion in gratitude to Guy run by his horses side like a trueborn spaniel, till lack of food made him retire to his wonted abode.[11]

Soon after Guy met with the Earl of Terry, whose father was confined in his castle by Duke Otto; but he and that lord posted thither, and freed the castle immediately; and Guy in an open field slew Duke Otto hand to hand; but his dying words of repentance moved Guy to remorse and pity.

But as Guy returned through a desart; he met a furious boar that had slain many Christians. Guy manfully drew his sword and the boar gaping, intending with his dreadful tusks to devour our noble champion; but Guy run it down his throat & slew the greatest boar that ever man beheld.

At Guy's arrival in England, he immediately repaired to King Athelstone, at York, when the King told Guy of a mighty dragon in

5.   Guy fights the dragon.

Northumberland, that destroyed men, women, and children. - Guy
desired a guide, and went immediately to the dragon's cave, when
out came the monster, with eyes like flaming fire; Guy charged him
courageously, but the monster bit the lance in two like a reed; then
Guy drew his sword, and cut such gashes in the dragon's sides, that
the blood and life poured out of his venemous carcase.

Then Guy
cut off the head of the monster, and presented it to the king, who in
memory of Guy's service caused the picture of the dragon being
thirty feet in length to be worked in cloth of arras, and hung up in
Warwick Castle for an everlasting monument.[12]

Phillis hearing of Guy's return and success, came as far as
London to meet him, where they were married with much joy and
triumph: King Athelstone, his queen the chief nobles and barons of
the land being present.

No sooner were their nuptials celebrated but Phillis's father
died, leaving all his estate to Sir Guy; and the king made him Earl
of Warwick.

CHAPTER V

Guy leaves his Wife, and goes a Pilgrimage to the Holy Land.

In the very height of Guy's glory, being exalted to all his father's
dignities, conscience biddeth him repent of all his former sins, and
his youthful time, spent in the behalf of women; so Guy resolved to
travel to the Holy Land like a pilgrim, Phillis, perceiving this
sudden alteration, enquires of her Lord what was the cause of this
passion? - Ah! Phillis, said he, I have spent much time in honouring
thee, and to win thy favour, but neverspared one minute for my
soul's health in honouring the Lord.

Phillis, though very much grieved, understanding his
determination, opposed not his will - so with exchanging their
rings, and melting kisses, he departed like a stranger, from his own
habitation taking neither money nor scrip with him, and but a small
quantity of herbs and roots, such as the wild fields could afford,
were his chief diet; vowing never to fight more but in a just cause.

Guy, after travelling many tedious miles, met an aged man oppressed with grief, for the loss of fifteen sons, whom Armarant, a might giant had taken from him, and held in strong captivity. Guy borrowed the old man's sword, and went directly up to the castle gate where the giant dwelt, who coming to the door, asked grimly, How he durst so boldly to knock at his gates? vowing he would beat his brains out. But Guy laughing at him, said Sirrah, thou art quarrelsome; - but I have a sword has often hewn such lubbards as you asunder: -

At the same time laying his blade about the giant's shoulders, that he bled abundantly, who being much enraged, flung his club at Guy, with such force, that it beat him down, and before Guy could recover his fall, Armarant had got up his club again, But in the end Guy killed this broad back'd dog, and released diverse captives that had been in thrawldom many years, some almost famished, and others ready to expire under various tortures. - They returned thanks to Guy for their happy deliverance; after which he gave up the castle and keys to the old man and his fifteen sons.[13]

Guy pursued his intended journey, and coming to a grave, he took up a wormeaten skull, which he thus addressed - Perhaps thou wert a prince, or a mighty monarch, a king, a duke, a lord! - But the beggar and the King must all return to the earth; and therefore man had need to remember his dying hour. Perhaps thou mightest have been a queen or a duchess, or a lady, garnished with meat lying in the grave, the sepulchre of all creatures.

While Guy was in this repenting solitude, fair Phillis, like a mourning widow, cloathed herself in sable attire, and vowed chastity in the absence of her beloved husband. Her whole delight was in divine mediations and heavenly consolations, praying for the welfare of her beloved lord, fearing some savage monster had devoured him. - Thus Phillis spent the remainder of her life in sorrow for her dear lord, and to show her humility, she sold her jewels and costly robes, with which she used to grace King Athelstones court, and gave the money freely to the poor; she relieved the lame and the blind, the widow and the fatherless, and all those that came to ask alms; building a large hospital for aged and sick people, that they might be comforted in their sickness and weak condition. - And according to this rule she laid up treasure in heaven, which will be paid again with life everlasting.[14]

Mean time Guy travelled through many lands and nations; at last in his journey he met the Earl of Terry, who had been exiled from his territory by a merciless traitor. - Guy bid him not be dismayed, and promised to venture his life for his restoration. The earl thanked Guy most courteously, and they travelled together against Terry's enemy, Guy challenged him into the field, and there slew him hand to hand, and restored the earl to all his lands.

The earl begged to know the name of his champion, but Guy insisted to remain in secret, neither would he take any gratuity for his services.

Thus was the noble Guy succesful in all his actions, and finding his head crowned with silver hairs, after many years travel, he resolved to lay his aged body in his native country, and therefore returning from the Holy Land, he came to England, where he found the nation in great distress, the Danes having invaded the land, burning cities and towns, plundering the country, and killing men, women and children; insomuch that King Althenstone was forced to take refuge in his invincible city of Winchester.

CHAPTER VI

Guy fights with the Giant Colborn, and having overcome him, discovers himself to the King; then to his wife and dies in her arms.

The Danes having intelligence of Athelstone's retreat to Winchester, drew all his forces thither, and seeing there was no ways to win the city, they sent a summons to King Athelstone, desiring that an Englishman might combat with a Dane, and that side to lose the whole whose champion was defeated.

On this mighty Colborn singled himself from the Danes, and entered upon Morn Hill, near Winchester, breathing venemous words, calling the English cowardly dogs, that he would make their carcasses food for ravens - What mighty boasting, said he, hath then been in the foreign nation of these English cowards, as if they

6.   Guy fights the giant Armarant.

had done their deeds of wonders, who now like foxes hide their heads.[15]

Guy hearing proud Colborn, could no longer forbear, but went immediately to the king, and on his knees begged a combat; the king liking the courage of the pilgrim, bid him go and prosper. - Guy walking out at the North Gate to Morn-Hill, where Colborn the Danish champion was. - When Colborn espied Guy, he disdained him, saying, Art thou the best champion England can afford? Quoth Guy it is unbecoming a professed champion to rail, my sword shall be my orator. No longer they stood to parley, but with great courage fought most manfully, but Guy was so nimble, that in vain Colborn struck, for every blow fell on the ground. Guy still laid about him like a dragon, which gave great encouragement to the English; but Colborn in the end growing faint, Guy brought, the giant to the Ground; upon which the English all shouted with so much Joy, that peals of echoes rung in the air. - After this battle the Danes returned into their own country.

King Athelstone sent for this champion to honour him, - but Guy refused honours, saying, My lege, I am a mortal man; and have set the vain world at defiance. But at the kings earnest request, on promise of concealment, Guy discovered himself to him, which much rejoiced his heart, and he embraced his worthy champion; but Guy took leave of his sovereign, and went into the fields where he made him a cave, living very pensive and solitary, and finding his hour drew near, Guy sent a messenger to Phillis, at the sight of which she hasted to her lord, where with weeping joy they embraced each other. - Guy departed this life in her arms, and was honourably interred.

His widow grieving at his death died fifteen days after him,

Their EPITAPH

Under this marble there lies a pair,
Scarce such another in the world there are,
Like him so valiant, like her so fair.
His actions thro' the world have spread his fame,
And to the highest Honours rais'd his name;

For conjugal affection, and chaste love,
She's only equalled by the blest above,
Below they all perfection did possess,
And now enjoy consummate happiness.

FINIS

Guy of Warwick
(Verse)

A
Remarkable Account
of GUY

Who, by strange enterprizes in war, obtained for his bride, PHELICE, the daughter of ROBAND, Earl of Warwick, and after he became the successor of Earl ROBAND, freely parted with scenes of worldly honor, and lived in poverty, and died in obscurity.

IN A POEM ENTIRELY NEW

IF we know not our own elevation rather by the mortification and denial of ourselves than by the multiplication of our devout exercises, it is to be feared they will be rather practices of condemnation than of sanctification.[1]
MONS. DE RENTY

Printed by
GEORGE J. OSBORNE
Gutemberg's Head, Newburyport

MDCCXCIII
1793

A Remarkable Account of Guy

Guy, with the beauty of fair Phelice charm'd,
With courage brave himself he nobly arm'd,
In war and dangers did expose his strength,
That he might gain her for his bride at length.
And when most dismal hazards he had run,
And for her sake had many battles won,
And had obtained her for his nuptial bride,
Soon took the earldom when Earl Roband dy'd.
But soon this scene of earthly bliss is gone,
When he his former life did think upon;
He sees those acts which gave him his renown,
He wickedly in heaven's sight had done.
Oft would he sit and meditate alone,
On those vain steps which rashly he had run;
Then by himself, with groans and bitter sighs,
O pardon me, just heav'n, would be his cries;
'Tis nothing I have done deserves thy grace,
For vainly I have gone in wicked ways,
Profusely I the blood of mortals shed,
All for the sake of one whom I did wed;
But never spent one weeping hour for sin,
'Tis now high time repentance to begin.
I now will spend the remnant of my days
In deep contrition for my former ways.
Unto the world I now will learn to die,
Tho' I it's censures do obtain thereby;
Altho' my youth ambitious pride has known,
I'll teach age meekness ere my glass be run;

And bid wealth, honour, beauty, all farewell,
And, to gain heav'n, would even pass thro' hell.

Phelice perceiving him disconsolate,
Inquires why he so changed is of late,
That as she in his joys a part did share,
She likewise of his sorrows part might bear.

Guy then to her reveal'd his mournful case,
How countless sins did stare him in the face,
And that he was resolved soon to leave
That wealth and ease their mutual friendship gave.
No more to share in worldly joy again,
But in contempt of worldly ease or pain,
Drest in a palmer's weed, and pilgrim's hue,
A tedious, obscure journey would pursue,
And gave his ring unto his lady fair,
Expressive of the love he to her bear;
Requesting her the same pledge to bestow,
And that till death it should not from him go.

Now Guy no more in princely garb appears,
But leaves fair Phelice in a flood of tears,
And straightways goes toward the Holy Land,
Where old Jerusalem's city once did stand.
Then Guy, who once in quarrels was so stout,
And for his Phelice rang'd the world about,
Resolves in his own cause no strokes to give,
Nor suffer malice in his heart to live,
Sometimes he search into a grave would make,
And out of it a dead man's skull would take,
And would a seeming converse with it hold,
As tho' to him it's vanity it told.
If thou hast been a monarch where's thy crown,
Or who from thee need fear an awful frown ?
Death hath of my renown a conquest made -
My golden sceptre now aside is laid,

And stript me of my honour - and my case
Is such, my subjects envy not my place.
If thou hast been some counsellor of state,
Where is thy wit which govern'd realms of late ?
Consum'd and gone, and now will not suffice
To rule the worms where my poor carcase lies.
Perhaps thou wast some charming lady fair,
And for thy sake some bold exploits done were,
Tho' comely features once might thee adorn,
But who can now beauty in thee discern ?
By powerful death it's turned to the dust,
Both loathsome and defil'd, thy beauty's lost,
And only a sad picture doth remain,
To tell the world that beauty's all in vain.

Such plain memento's he would of't prefer,
Which made the face of death to him appear
To teach the flesh how apt 'tis to mistake,
And trifle with repentance for its sake.
But knowing that his mortal day must soon
Be past, and that his glass was almost run,
He to his native land return'd again,
To end his days where first they did begin;
And did find out a solitary cave,
From whence he of his lady alms would crave,
Who of him would inquire if he did know
Her lord, who on a pilgrimage did go?
And tho' with grief he heard her sad complaint
He unto her would then no comfort grant,
By letting her a knowledge of him have,
That 'tis her lord who alms of her did crave,
But, weeping, he would from her to his cell
Return again, in solitude to dwell;
And still to keep in sight mortality,
A dead man's head would place before his eye
Saying, with thee I shortly shall abide -
I loathe the flesh to which my soul is ty'd.

As sickness now begins to seize my heart,
I know I quickly must by death depart;
And lest I suddenly my days should end,
I to fair Phelice now my ring will send.
Then by an herdsman he did send it straight,
As from a pilgrim lately at her gate.
When she the ring did from the herdsman take
She then of him did strict enquiry make,
To know the place where her dear Guy did dwell,
And for his convoy did reward him well.

There in the cave a sight she then obtain'd
Of Guy, who solitary there remain'd -
They met with tears, but they could not express
The anguish which their hearts did then possess.

At length the earl did from his silence break,
And mournfully he thus to her did speak;
Now, Phelice, you must take your leave of Guy,
Within your arms I do deserve to die.
Lately to me you gave alms at your gate,
'Tis blessedness to pity poor man's state.
Look not so strange, my dear, lament not so,
Your tears are needless, I don't want them now,
For I have flowing tears of true remorse,
To which my conscience now a witness is,
You do not weep because I weep no more,
But to behold me friendless, weak, and poor;
This is the place which I have sought my love,
Tho' sad few do seek celestial joys above;
The soul which would obtain eternal rest,
Must vanities and fading joys detest.
Were we but looking with eyes spiritual
We might discern that nothing here doth dwell,
But subtil devils seeking unawares
To ruin souls by bates, and traps, and snares.
O Phelice, I have spent youth, nature's day,

Upon your love my morning past away
And for my God old rotten age have kept,
The night of nature (at which then he wept)
O blessed Saviour, all my sins forgive,
A sense of them doth make my sould to grieve;
Forgive me, who so many men have slain,
That I fair Phelice might at last obtain.
Since to this cave I did myself betake,
I sought with God above my peace to make;
Against whom I have been by sins misled,
In number more than hairs upon my head.
And finding my poor body full of pain,
I do this for my last will now ordain,
Which, if I can, Phelice, I'll read to you,
Before I bid this mortal life adieu.

His last Will and Testament

E'EN in his sacred name, whose power great,
Did heav'n and earth, and all things else create,
As one who instantly is to depart,
I leave this world with a resigned heart.
My soul I give to him who gave it me;
Receive it, Jesus, I it trust with thee.
To death I owe this life, a feeble blast,
Which, when I've paid, then it's demand is past;
Life is a breath, a vapour which I owe,
And with that I had paid it long ago,
But to my comfort, I can truly say
That I am ready, should death call this day.
Unto the world that stock of wealth I owe
Which it by traffic did on me bestow:
Less of it would have given more content;
But now of all which unto me was lent,
Of worldy things I now must be left bare,
And one poor sheet is all that I require.
My sins I give (whose numbers do surmount

The strictest of arithmetic's account)
To him who made them loads to burden me,
Receive them, Satan, for they came from thee.
I give good thoughts, with all my virtuous deeds
To him from whom all which good proceeds,
Which I by grace have guided been unto,
For only evil I by nature do.
I own myself to be conceiv'd in sin,
That I was born and lived have therein.
My sinful life, while I did here remain,
I do consider as most vile and vain,
To sorrow I my sighs and tears impart,
Fetch'd from the bottom of a bleeding heart.
I give repentance, tears, and wat'ry eyes
Of a true convert, and unfeigned sighs;
And may the earth or sea a place provide,
Which for a grave may this vile body hide,
If Jesus doth but grant an heavenly place,
Where my poor soul may dwell before his face.

Phelice, I faint ! my loyal spouse, farewel,
With thee I trust in the blest world to dwell,
Where eyes with flowing tears no more shall grieve
Come, blessed Jesus, now my soul receive,
With these last words Death did his eyelids close,
While Phelice, nearly dead with grief and woes,
No [.....][2] could peace to her afford
She wet with tears her dear departed lord;
Beating her breast till breast and heart were sore,
Wringing her hands till she could strive no more,
Ah, cruel death! of all my grief the cause,
Give me a stroke which may requite my loss,
Let me not see to-morrow's dawning light,
But make me as this corpse now in my sight,
In which I do behold, most clear and plain,
The true description of a mortal man.
Kissing his face, while she in tears did swim,

76

She leaves his body for the grave to claim;
And from that place as sad a soul did bear,
As in her sex then ever did appear,
As full of grief as one could be alive,
But fifteen days she did her lord survive.

*The Seven Champions
of Christendom*

THE

HISTORY

OF THE

Seven Champions

of

Christendom

Containing, Their honourable Births, Victories, and noble
Atchievements by Sea and Land in divers strange Countries; their
Combats with Giants, Monsters, wonderful Adventures, Fortunes
and Misfortunes in Desarts, &c. Their Conquests of Empires and
Kingdoms, relieving distressed Ladies, &c. &c. Being both
pleasant and delightful

Salop: Printed by J. Cotton and J. Eddowes

The Seven Champions of Christendom

The Parentage and Birth of St. George; and how he was stole away by an Inchantress.

NOT long after the destruction of Troy,[1] sprung up the seven Wonders of the World, the Seven Champions of Christendom. St. George for England, St. Dennis for France, St. James for Spain, St. Andrew for Scotland, St. Anthony for Italy, St. Patrick for Ireland, St. David for Wales. St. George was born in the City of Coventry, and for his magnanimous deeds of arms in foreign adventures, had the title given him The Valiant Knight St. George of England; whose golden garter is still worn by kings, princes and noblemen, in memory of his many victories. When his mother was conceived of him, she dreamed she was with child of a dragon, whch should be the cause of her death: which dream she concealed till her painful burthen grew so heavy, her womb was not able to bear it; so that at length she revealed it to her husband, who was then Lord Steward of England. This doleful dream struck such terror into her husband's heart, that he was speechless; but recovering, he assured her that he would try the utmost that art and nature could do, to find out the meaning of the dream; and taking only one knight with him, goes to the solitary walks of Calyb, the wise Lady of the Woods, and taking a lamb to offer sacrifice to the inchantress with him, they came to an iron-gate, whereon hung a brazen horn for them to wind, that would speak with the inchantress: they first offered the lamb with great devotion before the iron-gate, and then without any fear they blew the brazen horn, the sound whereof made the earth to tremble; after which they heard a terrible voice out of the earth, uttering these words following:

Sir Knight begone and mark me well,
Within the lady's womb doth dwell,
A son, who like a dragon fierce,
His mother's tender womb shall pierce,
A valiant champion he shall be,
In noble acts and chivalry,
Begone, I now bid you adieu:
You'll find what I have told is true.

The dark riddle being thus repeated, so amazed them, that they thought to wind the horn a second time to know the meaning of it; but not daring to venture, they left the inchanted cave. In the mean time the lady had such a bitter labour, that either she or the child must perish; upon which, she for the good of her country, was content her tender womb should be opened, that the child might be taken out alive; so being cast into a dead sleep, the operation was made: He had on his breast the lively picture of a dragon, a blood-red cross on his right hand, and a gold garter on his left leg: they named him George, and provided him three nurses, one to give him suck, another to keep him asleep, and the third to provide him food; soon after his birth, the inchantress Calyb stole the noble infant from the careless nurses; the noble lord now returning, met with these two lamentable misfortunes, and sent messengers to all countries to find out his son, but could hear no tale nor tidings of him, which soon brought him to his grave.

The witch Calyb had detained St. George in her cave fourteen Years, and at length fell in love with him, which he declined, his mind being set upon martial adventures: Nevertheless hoping to obtain his liberty, if in case he made him master of that inchanted place, he seemed willing, and wound himself in by degrees to have her yield all her power over unto him, which she willingly did; and he intreated her to tell him of his birth, his name, and parentage: Thou art, quoth she, by birth, son to the Lord Albert, High-Steward of England, and from thy birth to this day, have I kept thee as my child, and my virginity for thee; so taking him by the hand, she led him into a brazen castle, wherein remained six of the bravest knights in the world: These are, said she, six worthy Champions of Christendom, the first is St. Dennis of France, the second St. James of Spain, the third St. Anthony of Italy, the fourth St. Andrew of Scotland, the fifth St. Patrick of Ireland, the sixth St. David of Wales, and thou art born to be the seventh, thy name being St. George of England, for so shalt thou be called in time to come; then taking him by the hand, she led him into a fair large room, where stood seven of the goodliest steeds that ever eye beheld; six of these, said she, belong to these six knights, and the seventh I will bestow upon thee, whose name is Bucephalus, the name of Alexander's great horse. Moreover, she led him into another room, wherein was the richest armour in the world, choosing out the strongest corslet from the armory, she with her own hands buckled it about his breast, laced on his helmet, and attired him with a rich caparison; then fetched forth a huge faulchion² and put into his hand: now, quoth she, thou art invincible, never to be conquered, for now hast thou the strongest armour in the world, and a sword shall cut the hardest flint asunder. Thus being blinded with her own lust, she put a silver wand in his hand, which wrought her own destruction; for then had he power of all the inchanted wood; so as they were walking along by a mighty rock, which the knight perceiving, struck with the silver wand, so that the rock opened, and there did he see before his eyes a number of little infants which she had murdered by her inchantment: St George, quoth she, I will shew thee more than this, if thou wilt follow me; so stepping in, he with his inchanted wand struck the rock again, and the rock closed her in, and there was the end of that famous inchantress, where we will leave her to the fury of the devils, and speak more of St. George, who released six champions out of captivity; they giving him many thanks, went with him to seek their fortunes, whose matchless deeds shall be shew'd in the following chapter.

How St. George killed the burning Dragon in AEgypt, and redeemed SABRA the King's Daughter from Death.

SOON after the Seven Champions departed from the inchanted cave of Calyb, and stayed a while in the city of Coventry, where they erected a stately monument in honour of St. George's mother, and in the beginning of spring they took their leaves one of another, and went each one a several way to seek their fortunes; where we shall leave the six champions to their contented travels, and discourse of our country-man, the chief of them. St. George of England, who travell'd till he came into the territories of AEgypt, where he found the people in sad distress, by reason of a fiery dragon, which every day devour'd a virgin; now the king had made proclamation thro' all his realm, that if any knight was so hardy as to encounter with this dragon and kill him, he should have his daughter in marriage, and the crown after his decease. Upon hearing of which, St. George resolved to venture his own life to set the lady free. Next morning, mounting his steed, he posted away to encounter with the fiery dragon, where upon the way, he overtakes the woeful virgin (the king's daughter) accompanied with a number of sorrowful matrons, bewailing her unfortunate fate. St. George comforts them up with these words:

> Fair Princess, and ye matrons all,
> Refrain, and mourn no more;
> For by the fiery dragon's fall,
> Your freedom I'll restore.
> The dragon is your enemy
> I'll quickly end the strife;
> I'll clip his wings, he shall not fly,
> Or George shall loose his Life.

The princess beholding St. George's courage, admired that he, being a stranger, should adventure himself for her sake, when the stoutest champions in AEgypt durst not.

> Sir Knight, I give you thanks, quoth she,
> That undertakes this fight;
> And since it is for love of me,
> The King shall you requite.
> And if you perish in this thing,
> The which you take in hand,
> Next comes the daughter of a king,
> As well you understand.
> Go forth, and prosper, worthy knight,
> And leave me sore perplext;

If you miscarry in the fight,
Then I must be the next.

St. George kissed the princess's hand, and vowed to free her, or lose his life; intreating the company to conduct her to her father's palace, till they heard further.

Now as St. George entered the valley, and came near to the cave, the dragon espied him, and sent forth such a terrible bellowing, as if all the devils in hell had been present. St. George was never a wit daunted, but spurred his horse and ran outragiously at him; but his scales being harder than any brass, he shivered his spear in a thousand pieces, and withal smote St. George so hard with his wings and tail, that he struck him down from his horse, and bruised him sore.[3] St. George then was forced to draw his sword, when began a most terrible fight between him and the dragon; and the good knight was almost poisoned with the breath of the dragon, so that he was forc'd to retire, and spying a fruit which no venemous thing durst come near, eat of the said fruit, and recovered again, and then with manly courage, assaulted the dragon in such sort, that he felled him under his horse's feet; the dragon recovering himself, lifted up his wings as if he intended to fly away, which St. George seeing, and espying a bare place under the dragon's wings, run his sword up to the hilt, which so pierced his heart, that with a terrible noise he breathed out his last breath, and yielded his life to the conqueror.

Thus was the land freed from this devouring monster, and the champion received with joy and gladness.

How St. Dennis of France lived seven Years in the Shape of a Hart. How proud Eglantine, the King's Daughter of Thessaly, was transformed into a Mulberry-Tree; and how they both recovered their Shapes by the Means of St. Dennis's Horse.

FAIR Eglantine, daughter of the King of Thessaly, for her pride was transformed into a mulberry-tree in the wilderness of Arabia. It was St. Dennis's fortune to travel thro' that unhappy place, where this unfortunate lady was transformed into a mulberry-tree, and

being almost starved, was forced to eat roots, or any wild fruit he
could find; and wandering about this desart, at length he came to
this mulberry-tree, where beholding some fruit on it began to eat;
and he no sooner had tasted of these berries, but he was translated
into a hart, where beholding himself in a spring, he began to bewail
himself in this manner:

> I was a man that fame did gain,
>   But now a hart in show;
> When I shall be a man again,
>   Alas! I do not know.

The voice in the mulberry-tree,

> Be patient now, brave knight, said she,
>   Thy case is just like mine:
> But you and I shall one day see,
>   Our honours both to shine.
> Seven years thou shalt continue so,
>   Hunger increase thy woes;
> At length thou shalt end all thy woe,
>   By eating of a rose.

When he had heard this voice, he stood much amazed and
speechless for sorrow, considering how long a time it would be e'er
he should return again to the society of men; but his speech getting
utterance, he thus bewail'd his misfortune:

O wretched creature and miserable (said he) how am I confined
in this solitary place, exposed to hardship and danger in the shape
of a beast; and subject to many misfortunes more than yet I know:
Accursed was the time I wandered to this unlucky place, to be
scorched by the sun's beams in summer, and wet with showers; and
in winter to have snow my covering, and no human food to sustain
me. Upon this, tears burst from his eyes, and sighs from his
afflicted breast; yet so inchanted he was, that he could not remove
from thence, nor cared he much to endeavour it, till his proper
shape returned, lest he should fall a prey to common hunters, which
he remembred was once Acteon's fate, so transformed by Diana for
presuming to see her bathing naked in a chrystal fountain: and it

more likewise grieved him that he could not be in arms to succour distressed ladies, and rid the world of oppressors and tyrants; yet was he compelled to bear all with as much patience as his fortitude could arm him with. All this while his gallant steed never left him, but grazed near him, sympathized with his master's sorrow, and brought him boughs, which he had plucked from the spreading trees with his teeth to make him a shelter; and thus it was with him, till seven summers and winters had passed over his head; then one morning as he was praying to heaven for mercy and deliverance, he perceived at a distance his horse labouring to climb up a steep rock; and having stayed a while there, he descended with a branch of a rose-tree, on which were three roses of Jerusalem; he had no sooner brought it to him, but he remembered the voice in the mulberry-tree; whereupon he greedily eat one of them, and reserved the rest, for fear the like danger might befall him, or any of the champions in other places. He had no sooner digested it, but his hair fell off and he assumed his manly shape, finding himself exceedingly refreshed.

Upon this he heard the voice of a woman weeping in the hole of the tree, intreating him to cut down the tree, and deliver her, for now the time was accomplished: With that remembring where he had laid his sword, he fetched it, and with divers violent blows, felled it out of the hollow, underneath which sprung a beautiful lady naked, whom he covered with his mantle, who made him great reverence, saying, her name was Eglantine, daughter to the King of Thessaly, who had been by inchantment, for her intollerable pride, confined to that place; then travelling in the most beaten paths, they found the way out of the wilderness; and she being mounted behind him, he conveys her to his father's court, where they were received with more joy and welcome, than I can express.

How St. James, the Champion of Spain, continued seven Years dumb for the love of a fair Jew; and how he was to have been shot to Death by the Maidens of Jerusalem: with other Things that happened in his Travels.

NOW St. James was minded to travel to Jerusalem; and passing over the confines of Sicily, near the burning lake, had a most terrible battle with a fiery drake for seven days and seven nights; he then passed thro' Cappadocia, then thro' a wilderness of monsters; at length came in sight of fair Jerusalem, which appeared to him the finest city in the world, inhabited by Jews; just at the time of his arrival, the king of the country, with all his knights in arms, prepared themselves for hunting; for the country at that time was much annoyed with wild beasts; as lions, bears, tygers, and such like; the trumpets sounding before them in such manner, as made the Spanish champion amazed; and wondering what the meaning should be, enquired of a shepherd, who told him, that the king and his nobles were intending that day to hunt, the country being much annoyed with wild beasts; and the king had made proclamation, that whoever killed the first boar, should be well rewarded. Away rid St. James, and was in the forest before them all; and by that time the king came, he had killed the greatest boar that ever mortal man beheld, who lived in a cave upon the flesh of people which he had slain; the king said he deserved the reward; but withal demanded what country-man he was, and of what religion. St. James said, he was a Spaniard by birth, and a Christian by profession. When the king heard that, he was wroth, and said thus unto him: Presumptuous Christian, didst thou never hear of the laws and customs of our nation, that what Christian soever dares approach into our confines, shall straitway be put to death? Yet in regard thou hast done good service for our country in destroying this wild boar, thou shalt have the favour to chuse thine own death. St. James admired that he should be so ill rewarded for his good service; yet seeing it was their law, and the king's pleasure it should be so, he chose to be shot to death with arrows, by the hands of a virgin.[1] Divers virgins were sent for, who, seeing St. James bound fast to a tree, with his breast naked to receive the shaft, beheld also his comely shape; and considering what good he had done for their country, in killing the wild boar that had destroyed so many, utterly refused the same; insomuch that the king commanded that they should cast lots, and on whom the lot fell, she should be his executioner: Lots were made, and the lot fell upon the king's own daughter. The fair princess, whose name was Cele, no sooner beheld his manly admirable beauty, but love seized her tender breast; she cast the bow and arrow out of her hand, and falling on her knees before her father, begged for his life in these terms:

Great Sir, if ever pity moved your breast, behold with compassion the tears of your most obedient daughter on her bended knees, and grant my request.

What is it? said he.

Ah! replied she, that this worthy champion, this man, whose fame is spoken of loud through the world, may not be basely slain. How ungrateful it will be in the ears of all nations, when it is told, you have murdered so brave a knight, who had ventured his life in rescuing your country from its bloody enemy.

Well, said the king, since you have interceded for him, I cannot deny his life to your tears: But this is an unalterable decree, that he be banished the territories of India,[5] as an enemy to our country; and he shall surely die, if ever he return again.

At this she was exceeding sad, but could not further prevail; so rising, she went and unbound him with her fair hands, saying, Most noble knight, I have gained your life and liberty, yet cannot prevail that you may stay in this land, though I most earnestly desire your company; since in your absence I must be as one banished, without peace or rest. Let my blushes excuse me when I tell you I love you, and let not the forwardness of a virgin make you the less value her, who can no longer stifle her passion.

The noble knight received the knowledge of her love, in the most obliging terms, being at the same time struck with the like passion for her: he kissed her hand, stiling her, his deliverer, vowing to her perpetual love and constancy; promising, though now her father's rigid and unjust sentence forced him away, he would e'er long return and convey her to his country; so, with a tender kiss she slipped a diamond ring on his finger; then they parted, but not without tears in their eyes. The Spanish champion riding some miles, alighted to rest himself on the edge of a forest, and there began to think his honour would suffer through imputed fear, in his so tamely leaving his lovely princess; wherefore, he resolved to return to the court in disguise, and that his speech should not betray him, to feign himself dumb. This he put in practice, and was, in the disguise of an Indian, received into the king's service: The princess for the noble spirit she saw in him, tho' in that disguise she knew him not, appointed him her champion in all cases; when so it happened, that Nabuzaradam King of Arabia, and the Calif of Babylon came to court; both fell desperately in love with her, striving with musick and singing who should get most in her favour, and made their presents to her, which were very rich; St. James making his likewise, (being one amongst them) slipt the diamond ring into her hand; which knowing, she retired to her chamber, and sent for him, where he discovered himself, to her great joy; so it was contrived between them, whilst the court was busy in revelling, to make their escape; which they did on swift horses that night, and after long travel, to their great satisfaction they arrived safe in Spain.[6]

How St. Anthony slew a Giant, and released many Ladies out of Captivity. How St. Andrew travelled thro' a Vale of walking Spirits. How St. Patrick redeemed six Thracian Ladies from thirty Satyrs, and of their Travel to find out the champion of Scotland. How St. David slew Count Palatine; and how he was sent to the inchanted Garden of Ormandine, where he slept seven Years and was redeemed by St. George.

St. Anthony, after his passage through many dangerous places, came to the top of a mighty mountain, whereon stood a castle; within this castle remained a mighty giant, who for strength no man durst encounter; this giant kept within his castle the seven daughters of the King of Thracia, wherein six of them were transformed into swans with crowns on their heads, because they would not yield to the lust of the giant; the other remained with him to play and sing him asleep. This great giant St. Anthony slew, and left the castle to them, whereby their father the King might have access to them, as you shall hear hereafter.

The famous Champion St. Andrew of Scotland, travelled thro' a vale of walking spirits, most fearful to behold, and had not seen the light of the sun for seven days, but was only guided by a walking fire, till he came to a castle, before which lay the giant that St. Anthony slew; his flesh rent and torn by wild foxes, crows and such like. The champion entered the castle, where he found the King of Thracia, bewailing his daughters' ill fortune, with many of his nobility with him, calling upon their gods in behalf of his daughters; which when St. Andrew saw, he smiled, and said unto the king, If you will believe in the Christians' God, and call upon him with me, your daughters shall be restored to their former shapes again. No sooner had he spoke, but they all drew their swords and run upon him altogether, insomuch that they put St. Andrew hard to it; nevertheless, after a very hot dispute St. Andrew overcame them, and the king himself lay at his mercy, who presently turned Christian. He and all his followers then calling on the Lord of Hosts, suddenly the King of Thracia's daughters were restored again to their former shapes, being more beautiful than ever they were before: Which mercy, when the king saw, he continued a Christian to his dying-day. But when the king and his daughters came to court, all their joy was turned to sorrow, for the champion of Italy, who slew the giant, had stole away the king's daughter, fair Rosalinde, and all the country was up in arms in pursuit of him, which when St. Andrew understood, he departed privately, and the king's daughters, understanding that he was gone, travelled after him, knowing under God, that he was the cause of their delivery out of bondage.

These six daughters of the King of Thracia, travelled until they came to Ireland, hoping to find the champion of Scotland; but instead of finding him, they met with thirty wild and cruel satyrs, who hauled them thro' woods and groves, and tore and rent them in such a grievous sort, that forced them to cry out in a most lamentable manner, so that the woods and all the country did ring of their pitiful cries. St. Patrick, who all this while was wandering about the country, stood amazed, and drawing his sword, ran up to the top of a high hill, where he beheld a lamentable spectacle, thirty terrible satyrs, with clubs on their shoulders, dragging these fair ladies by the hair of the head; he resolved to free them, or lose his life. He went forwards towards them in this manner Ladies, quoth he, be of good comfort, for I intend, if God be so pleased, to free

you; whereupon he let fly at them in such sort, that he slew the
chiefest of them, which made the rest take to their heels and run
away. St. Patrick demanded of those virgins who they were? They
told him, they were the King of Thracia's daughters; and how they
were for seven years kept in captivity by a mighty giant, and
transformed into swans by Diana, the Goddess of Chastity, to keep
and preserve them from the insatiate lust of the giant; and how their
eldest sister remained a pure virgin with the giant, until St.
Anthony came and slew the giant, freed their sister, and carried her
to the court of their father, who with a great number of knights
came to see him, and bewailed their sad condition, who were all
swimming in a pond in the shape of swans, with crowns of gold
upon their heads, to shew they were the daughters of a king.[7] In this
state they remained till St. Andrew came by, who restored them to
their former shapes again. When St. Patrick heard this, he said,
Worthy Ladies, these two champions are my friends, whom I have
not seen these seven years; as for St. Andrew of Scotland, whom
you seek, I will accompany you in the search of him. - Where we
will leave them, and speak something of St. David, the Champion
of Wales.

St. David of Wales, travelling to the Emperor of Tartary's
court, performed such gallant deeds of arms, that the emperor made
him his chief champion; where upon a festival day, the emperor
desirous of sport, caused tilt and tournament to be used. Now St.
David being the emperor's champion, entered the list first; so, the
emperor's son, being Count Palatine, ambitious of honour, came
straitway to answer him, and performed honourable deeds against
St. David the Champion of Wales; for the first encounter he had
almost thrown him off his horse to the ground; where the emperor's
son, the Count Palatine, was so bruised with the fall, that in a short
time after he died. This so enraged the emperor, that he plotted all
he could to make him away; nevertheless, he being well beloved of
all the court, the emperor could not without loss of honour do it;
but in regard St. David was his champion, he sent him to the
inchanted garden, to bring him the head of Ormandine the
inchanter; St. David durst refuse nothing the emperor enjoined him;
so he went with an undaunted courage, and found a sword fastened

to a rock, upon the pummel whereof was written, He that can pull me out, shall conquer all; St. David assailed to do it, but not being able, fell asleep for the space of seven years, till St. George at last came by the inchanted garden, pulled out the sword, and freed St. David; for by that means the inchanter died, and the inchanted garden vanished,

St. George, the worthy English champion, after escaping many dangers abroad, found an unkind destiny too fatally awaited him at home; for having a while lived a contemplative life, he intended to spend the rest of his days in penitence. The king sent to inform him, that a dreadful dragon, near Dunsmore, who had a mighty cave for her habitation, destroyed all the country about, so that men and cattle were daily devoured; against this monster, for his country's safety, the champion immediately took his way, and in a terrible combat slew him. For which deliverance, bells rung, and bonfires blazed throughout the kingdom: but this, to the noble champion was the most fatal of all his encounters; for the vast quantity of poison thrown upon him by the monstrous beast, (he now fighting without his shield) so infected his vital spirits, that two days after, he died in his own house, having charged his sons, who were by this time returned from seeking adventures, to follow his steps in virtue and heroick deeds; recommending them likewise to the king's care, who was then present, and afterwards prefered them to the chiefest offices and trusts in his kingdom.

St. George was buried in the chapel which yet bears his name at Windsor; his effigies, killing a dragon, is given as the English badge of honour to our own nobles; but the greatest princes abroad, are proud to be companions of it, or the Noble Order of the Garter.

> Thus weary with long travel, thro' great deeds,
> For tired fancy there some respite needs;
> So hoping it will give you all content,
> Because however it is took, it was well meant.

FINIS

At J. COTTON'S and J. EDDOWES'S, Booksellers in Shrewsbury; Travellers may be furnished with the following sorts of Histories, New and Old Ballads, &c.[8]

ACademy of Compliments:
Capt. Hind.
Robinson Crusoe.
Seven Champions.
Courtier and Tinker. Cookery Book.
Dreams and Moles.
Friar Bacon. Fairy Tales.
Friar and Boy 2 Parts.
Fortunatus.
Fortune Book.
Guy of Warwick.
Honest John and loving Kate 2 Parts.
Jack Horner.
Jack and Giants, 2 Parts.
King and Cobler, 2 Parts.
Lawrence Lazy.
Mother Bunch, 2 Parts.
Mother Shipton.
Patient Grissel. Parents best Gift.
Preparation for Heaven.
Riddles. Robin Hood.
Sir Richard Whittington.
Tom Thumb, 2 Parts (in one).
Tom Tram, 3 Parts.
Valentine and Orson. &c. &c. &c.

Parismus

THE
HISTORY
OF
PARISMUS,
THE
Valiant Prince of *BOHEMIA*:

CONTAINING

His Triumphant Battles fought againſt the *Perſians*, his Love to
the Beautiful Princeſs *Laurana*, the great Dangers he paſſed in the *Iſland
of Rocks*, and his ſtrange Adventures in the *Deſolate Iſland*
Together with the Adventures, Travels, and noble Chivalry of *Pariſmenos*
the *Knight of Fame*, with his Love to the Fair Princeſs *Angelica*, the
Lady of the Golden Tower.

Licens'd and Enter'd according to Order.

London : Printed by T. Norris, at the Looking glaſs on London-bridge

7. The title page of *Parismus*.

The title page of *Parismus* showing the printing details and cuts of a lady and
gentleman in late seventeenth-century costume. Some cuts in *Parismus* are
very closely related to events in the narrative, although they vary stylistically
but some (e.g. the storm, the tournament, the battle, the banquet) are almost
certainly drawn from Norris's general stock.

THE

HISTORY

OF

PARISMUS

THE

Valiant Prince of BOHEMIA:

CONTAINING

His Triumphant Battles fought against the Persians, his Love to the
Beautiful Princess Laurana, the great Dangers he passed in the
Island of Rocks, and his strange Adventures in the Desolate Island
Together with the Adventures, Travels, and noble Chivalry of
Parismenos the Knight of Fame, with his Love to the Fair Princess
Angelica, the Lady of the Goldrn Tower.
Licens'd and Enter'd according to Order

London: Printed by T. Norris, at the Looking glass on London-
bridge

The History of Parismus

CHAPTER I

How Parismus, Prince of Bohemia, arrived in Thessaly, and by the assistance of his friend Oristus, got a sight of the Princess Laurana, &c.

Parismus, son and heir to the King of Bohemia, having given at home sufficient proof of his courage, began to think of manifesting it abroad; and led by the fame of Laurana, daughter of Dyonisius, King of Thessaly, he determin'd to visit the court of Thebes, the metropolis of that country: where being receiv'd with all imaginable civility and magnificence, he aesolv'd to spend some time, with hopes of enjoying the beloved Laurana. Nor was he the only person that entertain'd those hopes, for as the world was fill'd with reports of her beauty and vertues, so was her father's court with princes, in hopes of gaining her affections. Amongst whom was Sicanus, Prince of Persia, who, with the King and Queen of Hnngary, Prince of Sparta, and Lady Isabella, came thither upon the same account. Dyonisius, famous as well for his hospitality, as the beauty of his daughter, entertain'd them with like courtesie: but Laurana, who had observ'd the two princes severally at their approach, conceiv'd an inclination, rather to like Parismus than Sicanus; not knowing either their business or their qualities, but seeing Parismus enter the palace, being a prince of comly gesture, she could not refrain from calling Leda, her maid to the chamber-window, to ask her opinion, concerning him; not from speaking many things in commendation of him. No sooner had he withdrawn, and enter'd the palace; but Laurana began to find in herself a sensible alteration; sometimes she blusht, as if in fault,

The Hiftory of *Parifmus*, &c.

Chap. I. *How* Parifmus, *Prince of* Bohemia, *arrived in* Theff:ly, *and by the Affiftance of his Friend* Oriftus, *got a fight of the Princefs* Laurana, *&c.*

8.   Parismus walking below Laurana's window.

Note that Parismus appears to be wearing classical dress.

and then presently look'd pale, for fear of being discover'd; sometimes she sigh'd, which she endeavour'd to drown in a cough; and sometimes study'd, which she always put off with a smile: This diversity of passions she no more knew how to prevent, than to guess at the cause: but Leda, being an experience'd amorist, soon guest at the distemper by the symptoms, and tho' she seem'd to discern nothing, yet she easily found all the tokens of an ensuing fit of love.

Dyonisius in the mean time entertaining the young princes, and nobles with all the splendor of his court, (expecting the fair Laurana) gave them all the satisf ction[1] they could wish or imagine; only Parismus, fill'd with the expectation of so divine a creature, could take delight in none of all the costly delicacies there provided: Which, while the other guests most lavishly devour'd, he cautiously fed himself even with more despair of seeing Laurana. However, he seem'd to do like the rest, that so his concernment might not be misconstrued, as an effect of his dislike; not truly construed, for an effect of his love. Dinner being ended, the company retir'd into the gardens, which were most sumptuous and delightful, as well for use as ornament, and fraught with all manner of fruits to please the palate, as well as flowers to gratify the other senses. Here, while the rest were diverting themselves according to their several inclinations, Parismus, singling out his friend Oristus, took him aside to a private walk in the wilderness, and there, after some questions about indifferent matters, he came to ask him how he liked the cours of Dyonisius, and whether those gardens were not much more pleasant than any in Bohemia? &c. To all which Oristus having answer'd in such a manner, ask he thought might best please the prince, he at last desired pardon of him if he likewise might presume to ask his Highness one question; to whom Parismus reply'd, An innocent question can offend none but a churlish disposition though propounded by an enemy, or stranger; much less from a bosom friend.[2] The replied Oristus, is not my lord in trouble of mind that he hath not yet enjoy'd the sight of the princess ? To whom Parismus replied, My dear friend, thou art so much the partaker of my heart, that I can keep no secret from thee; and when for a time I endeavour to be so unkind, my very self discovers that which I endeavour to conceal. 'Tis that which disquiets me, and takes from me the beauty of those delightful gardens, and indeed, of every place where she is not, or at least, not to be seen. Oristus perceiving him grow into a kind of amorous extacy, desired him to mitigate his passion, and question'd not by the interest he had in the Lord Remus (a great favourite) to procure him, not only the sight, but the speech of the admired lady; which for the present gave him some satisfaction, being willing to believe what he so much desired, tho' at present he saw no way how it might probably be effected. The evening wasting with many delightful and princely exercises, they began to think of repairing every one to their respective lodg ngs, where they were severally attended; and tho' the apartment allotted for Parismus were more richly adorned than any of the rest, yet such was his disquiet of mind, notwithstanding the comfort Oristus gave him, he took little rest that night, but spent the solitary hours in contemplation of a person he had never seen, and in framing for her such features as were best pleasing to himself.

Early in the morning Dyonisius, according to his custom, rose to go a hunting; and visiting his guests of chiefest note, desired their company; but Oristus purposing to perform his promise, stay'd behind with the Lord Remus, who invited him to take a walk in the gardens, and view the magnificent height and spacioas circumference of the place; which, whn Oristus had sufficiently admir'd; as they were returning, they were happily met by the illustrious Laurana, who with her maid, was coming to take the air, at a time she thought all the strangers of the court had been a hunting; she at first started to see the strange knight, but seeing the Lord Remus, she came on and said, I thought, my lord, this fine morning would certainly have drawn you into the field, who have always been a profest sportsman. Truly, Madam, said he, were I always sure to be blest with a sight of my princess, I should prove a very lazy huntsman; I confess, I did not intend at this time my self so great a happiness, but stay'd in civility to this gentleman who had otherwise been alone; so having kiss'd her hand, she welcom'd him to court, and pursu'd her walk. Now Oristus being inform'd by the Lord Rems of her apartment, he took particular notice thereof, and so left the garden. The king and train returning about noon, Parismus, who took but small delight in the pastime, comes with impatience to enquire of Oristus what news, whether he had seen his fair one; or discover'd her apartment? But Oristus, desiring his highness, to be a little patient, and not ask two questions, before he had answer'd one, gave him a full account of all that had happen'd, with such high commendations of the princess, as had been flattery of any other. With what joy Parismus heard him, let the reader judge; and yet no way satisfy'd, he almost envy'd his friend so great an happiness. However, being certified of her lodging, he resolved to walk there, in hopes of blessing his eyes with so divine a spectacle; In prosecution of which design, taking a book out of his pocket, and dismissing Oristus, he immediately repaired to the tarras-walk³, just under her chamber; and there made several turns, casting an eye much oftner towards her window than towards the volume he had in his hand, as hoping ineed to see there much the fairer impression; Laurana opening the casement, and not seeing the prince, gave him the full view of her face, which sight he so eagerly enjoyed, that he had almost lost himself with admiration. But to keep the prince from surfeiting, she had no sooner espy'd there a strange knight, but she immediately clapt to the casement, and thro' the crevices thereof, gave herself that satisfaction she deny'd him; who understanding by Oristus that the king waited his company at dinner, was forc'd to quit the walk, and brake himself to a banquet far less delightful that what he there enjoyed: The greatest part of dinner-time he spent in contemplation of his late happy success in the enjoying the sight of his beloved; the rest he imployed in contriving how he might come to the speech of her; which having modelled according to his fancy, he rose as it were abruptly from the table, and withdrawing himself to his quarters, sent an excuse to the king by one of his servants, desiring his majesty's gracious pardon of his rude departure, which he hoped the indisposition of his body would excuse. Dyonisius concern'd for the prince's sickness, as soon as dinner was ended, went to give him a visit, which Parismus suspecting, he set a page at his chamber-door to acquaint his majesty, or any else that should come

The History of Parismus and Parismenos.

Chap. II. *How* Parismus *discover'd his Love to* Laurana *at a Masque ; who (to the'r great Disquiet) is promised by the King her Father, in Marriage to his Rival* Sicanus, *Son to the Emperor of* Persia ; *Letters that passed between* Parismus *and* Laurana *and the jealous Envy of* Sicanus.

9.   The masque.

there, that he was in a slumber, and desired not to be disturbed. This excuse gave Dyonisius satisfaction for the present, and Parismus opportunity to carry on the design of seeing his mistress, unsuspected, which he effected in manner following:

CHAPTER II

How Paiismus dlscoover'd his love to Laurana at a masque; who (to their great disquiet) is promised by the King her father, in marriage to his rival Sicanus, son to the Emperor of Persia; letters that passed between Parismus and Laurana and the jealous envy of Sicanus.

Having understood from his friend Oristus, by information of the Lord Remus, that this was Laurana's birth-day, and that the Queen Olivia had order'd a royal banquet to be prepar'd for the entertainment of her princely guests, at which Laurana was to appear in publick (which she never did, but upon such occasions) Parismus projected with Oristus, and some other of the Bohemian court, to entertain the company with a mask, hopng by that device to attain to the speech of the incomparable Laurana, gave infinite satisfaction to the partakers. And now the company of the Bohemian prince seem'd only to be wanting to make their happiness compleat, especially to the inestimable princess, who not daring to make an enquiry, wondred that among so many worthy knights she could not espy the princely countenance of that gallant person she had the same day seen walking in the terras. While she was in these contemplations, notice was given, that a set of masquers were entring to divert the royal assembly, which after preparation made, were admmitted accordingly, and entred in this manner: first entred two Moors in white satin, with torches; and after them as many eunuchs in cloath of gold, playing on wind-mnsick[4]; then appeared the illustrous Parismus in a most beautiful disguise, dancing a sarabrand; next after him followed Oristus, and after him the Lord Remus, with two other knights of the Bohemian court, all most richly apparelled, and yet performing their several parts to admiration: But so infinite and surpassing was Parismus, as well in the shape of his body, as the excellency of his motion, that he attracted the eyes of all spectators especially hers, whom he most regarded, the matchless Laurana's: To whom in a submissive manner he addressed himself, and took her out to dance; Lord Remus took out the Lady Isabella, Oristus another Spartan lady, &c. so that altogether dancing a figure-dance, the resting-time and intervals Parismus imployed in making himself known to the lady of his affections. The masque ending with the applause of every juditious and Impartial eye, Dyonisius addrest himself to the masquers, returning them hearty thanks for the diversion they had given them, and desiring them to accept of a small banquet his daughter had prepared for them on her birth-day.[5] This Parismus accepted of with humble thanks, not so much for the sake of the banquet, but as for her that prepar'd it. And therefore to keep the king no longer in suspence, he pull'd off his vizard, and discoverd himself to be the Bohemian prince. Parismus! said the king smiling, I am glad you are so soon recovered: But now I see the cause of your distemper, and so cease to wonder at your sudden sickness, and departure from dinner. Which Parismus again excusing, and salating the whole company, than all applauded his princely behaviour, and courteous ingenuity, except the malicious Sicanus, who immediately quitted the room with an apparent shew of dislike. The rest of the company with drawing in to the banqueting-house at the request of Olivia, where they were again most magnificently treated with such delicacies as the ingenuity of Laurana could invent; with which tho' Parismus was highly pleased, he could not forbear looking very frequently upon Laurana; by which means, tho' he satisfied his own curiousity, he robbed the poor princess of many opportunities of viewing her Parismus: Nevertheless she had sometimes the luck to steal a glance as she thought, undiscern'd by any; tho' at the same time the whole company observ'd it, which caused many nobles, especially the friends of Sicanus, to envy the private kindness Laurana seemed to have for the Prince of Bohemia; of which, when they were departed, every one began to make their several constructions. Thus was Parismus and Laurana mutually enamour'd of each other, as it were at first interview, and when they got to their several quarters, seperately conspired to bring a bout ihe⁶ same end, viz. The farther enjoyment of each others company; the care of which Laurana committed to Leda the cabinet of he secrets; and Parismus to his trusty friend Oristus, with whom he consulted about the same matter.

Sicanus in the mean time freting with himself to see the Princess Laurana shew more favour to the Prince of Bohemia, than with the heir of Persia openly declared to Dyonisius, the cause of his coming was, to demand the Princess in marriage; the King of Hungary and Prince of Sparta, being come as embassadors upon the same account. To whom Dyonisius made answer, That for his part he should be very glad to have his daughter married to so hopeful a prince, and himself allay'd⁷ to so mighty an emperovr; promising with to propose the same to Laurana, who, he doubted not, would readily enough consent to so honourable a marriage. The princess all this while little imagining what mischief was plotting against her, spent the night in contriving which way she might again enjoy the sweet society of her beloved Parismus, who had now disquiet in casting about how to come into the company of his Laurana, but early in the morning geeting out of his bed, attiring in a careless, but comely dress, he repaired again to the old terras walk, as the only expedient he could think of to that purpose. He had not taken many turn, but Laurana had spied him tho' the glass and dispatching her maid Leda upon some sleeveless errand into the garden, she concluded Parismus would have something to say to her, which might be to her satisfaction. And accordingly it fell out, for as Leda was gathering a nose-gay of rhe prettiest and choicest flowers, Parismus, saluted her with a courteous good-morrow, and demanded how fared her lady the princess: who returning him thanks for his kind enquiry, satisfied him that she was in good health; I pray you damsel, said he, present her with this paper, and the service of one Parismus; if it may not be too great a presumption in me, nor too great a trouble to yourself. I am confident, said Leda, no message from your highness will ever be look'd upon as a presumption by the princess, or seem a trouble to your unworthy servant; whereupon sliding intoher⁸ hand a present of no small value, he dismissed her, and again, betook himself to his walk in expectation of the event. Laurana having observed Parismus to give Leda a paper, imagin'd it was for herself, and be ng impatient to see the contents, met her at the stair-foot, and suddenly breaking it open, she read these words:

Most excellent Madam,
If the contents of this paper be a presumption it is the excess of my love that has occasion'd it; so that my fault must be my excuse; But if love be a faul, how great a criminal is Parismus? Pardon me, Madam, that I dare be so confident once more to beg the favour of kissing your royal hand, at such a time and place as your Highness shall think most convenient; for since the unhappy minute of your departure, I have not enjoy'd the least thought to my satisfaction, but the remembrance of having once seen you, and the resolution of ever being, Madam, Yours at command,
Parismus.

Laurana, glad at so fair an opportunity, at the same time to oblige a man that loved her, and enjoy the company of him she loved, thought no time like the present to give him an answer, and observing him to walk under the window in seeming expectation thereof, sent him this short reply:
Most Noble Prince,

I look upon your love to be like your self, honourable; and if so, neither is in it self a fault, nor tender it presumption: My maid will tell you at what time and place, you may expect to meet me, which is an argument of the confidence reposed in you, by
Laurana

Joyful at this receipt of this welcome and unexpected answer, Parismus thought himself amply recompenced for the misfortune he conceiv'd to himself in not having blest his eyes with the sight of the angelical Laurana; and having humbly returned his serviee by Leda, he made haste to his friend Oristus, as well to acquaint him of the happiuess that had befallen him, as to avoid the censure of suspitious eyes, who might otherwise guess at his design in walking under Laurana's window; for by this time every body was stirring, and Dponisius had sent for his daughter in order to the forementioned match of Sicanus, Laurana coming wi h all submission to know the pleasure of her king and father was soon welcomed with the unwelcome news of Sicans's love, which Dyonisius propos'd with all the seeming advantages that could be imagined, but in so mild a manner, that he seemed not to use the authority of a king, but the indulgence of a father; insomuch that though the thing propos'd was most unwelcome to her ears, she received the same with as obedient sweetness, as if she had been ready to grant her consent: Whereupon Dyonisius, leaving Laurana to consider of it, went to Sicanus, and gave him all imaginable encouragement, making that day a general entertainment on purpose that Sicanus might find an opportunity of expressing his love to Laurana. Dinner being ready, it fortun'd that Parismus was seated just opposite to the princess, and Sicanus a pretty way below on the same side, so that while the one had the opportunity of viewing her perfection in their most resplendent lustre, the other had only now and then a side-view of her face; and while Parismus entertained her with pleasing (but common) discourse, Sicanus was so imprudent to imagine he had been making love: Thus did his gall boyl within him for the malice he bore to Parismus, against whom he vow'd perpetual enmity from that very hour. Nevertheless, after dinner, by the king's means he found an opportunity of discoursing Laurana, and manifesting his passion after the best manner he could, but so short it came of that vigour and sincerity she discerned in the love of Parismus, that in spight of her courteous and obliging nature, she was forced to receive it with a civil indifference, and to quit his company in a manner little better than scornful.

CHAPTER III

How Sicanus hired three Tartarians to murther Parismus, with the discovery thereof; Sicanus's flight: How Dyonisius, as a pilgrim, travels to Bohemia, and at last declares himself to Parismus's father.

Parismus little imagining what had past, began with some impatience to expect the happy hour of Laurana's appointment, (which being come, and the two lovers met accordingly, we will leave them in the arbour in mutual (but honourable) embraces, and speak a little of the malice and treason of Sicanus, who the same evening calling to him three Tartarians of his vassalage, after a great injunction of secrecy, and promise of a reward, made them swear to kill Parismus at a time they should find most convenient, which he doubted not to bring to pass in few days. All things being agreed upon, Sicanus betook himself to rest; and poor Parismus having by this time taken his unwelcome leave of the princess repaired likewise to his chamber, where, having taken rest proportionable to the comfort he received from the princess, he was ready with the earliest the next morning to go a hawking, it being a match of Sicanus his making, on purpose to draw him into the field, but the morning proving somewhat hazy, and unfit for that kind of exercise, most of the company would have put off the match till another day; but so importunate was Sicanus, that in complaisance to his humour they must go, tho' many of them (especially Parismus much against their wills; they had but little pastime all the morning, till at last springing an eye of pheasants in a large champaign, they flew a cast of goshawks, one of them immediately took a young pult⁹ at the pounce, the other undertaking the old hen, flew her into a large wood at a great distance under the wind; this none observed but Parismus, who rode up on Speedand was followed by the Tartarians; who taking that opportunity, unarm'd as he was, and dismounted in the thickest of the wood, fell upon him, and gave him many wounds, one of which in humane reason, had been enough to have destroyed the stoutest heart breathing; at last concluding he was fully dead, they buried him with leaves and moss, and return'd unsuspected to the company.

Sicanus, the bloody author of all this villainy, dissembled as much grief for the loss of Parismus as any of the rest, and having rewarded the barbarous Tartarians with a thousand crowns, he began to think of himself as secure from discovery, as he was free from suspition; but so it happened, that the villains disagreeing about dividing the money, one of them struck the other so mortal a stroke, that in short time he died thereof, but upon his death-bed confessed to Oristus the manner of Parismus's end; as also, that himself, with two others were hired by Sicanus to that purpose. Oristus repaired immediately to Sicanus; and in presence of the king taxed him with his reason, to which having little to say, he immediately drew a dagger, and had like to have slain his just accuser: Whereupon there grew a tumult betwixt the Persian and Bohemia knights, which Dionysius himself had much ado to appease. At last, Sicanus, betwixt fear and shame, having lost three of his followers in the skirmish, quitted the court, and fled into his own country, resolving to return with power, and demand the lady, he had not rhetorick enough to persuade.

Dionysius putting all things together, considering the slender account he should be able to give the King of Bohemia for the murder of Parismus, in suffering the author thereof to escape out of his court, took upon the habit of a pilgrim, and went disguised into Bohemia, to find in what manner the king resented the death of his son. Hence began new troubles in the court of Thebes, for missing the king at dinner, Olivia sent messengers every way to seek him, who many times met him, but could never find him, for they enquired for him of himself. Dionysius after some days arrived in Bohemia, took him a poor lodging near the court, whither he daily resorted, and heard sad complaints for the loss of Parismus, but still with respect to the court of Thebes, and the hospitality of Dionysius. But after some days being mistrusted by the landlord for some greater person than he appeared, it was thought fit to acquaint the secretary therewith, who imagining he might be some spy caused him to be brought before the king: Whereupon desiring audience in private, he was forced to unbosom himself to his majesty, declaring his great sorrow for the death of Parismus, and desiring his majesty's gracious assistance in revenging so horrid a murder upon Sicanus, the author thereof. The King of Bohemia having recovered himself out of the surprise he was in at first, embraced Dionysius, and promised him his utmost assistance; whereupon he was prevailed with to stay in Bohemia certain days.

10.   The murder of Parismus and the search for his body.

Chap. IV. Sicanus *Invades* Theffaly ; *the King of* Bohemia *and* Hungary *came to relieve it ; The wonderful Exploits of the* Black Knight : *The Fortune of the War referr'd to a Combat, which the* Black Knight *by a Letter promifes to undertake on the behalf of* Laurana.

11. A battle showing phalanxes of pikemen and musketeers.

By the time that *Parismus* was printed this style of warfare would have been about sixty years out of date.

112

CHAPTER IV

Sicanus invades Thessaly; the King of Bohemia and Hungary came to relieve it; The wonderful exploits of the Black Knight: The fortune of the war referr'd to a combat, which the Black Knight by a letter promises to undertake on the behalf of Laurana.

SIcnaus being returned into Persia, complained of divers injuries and affronts offered him in the court of Dionysius, whence he hardly escaped with the loss of three of his attendants; whereupon he desired the king his father to levy forces, and go against Dionysius, to revenge the wrong he had done him. The king giving credit to Sicanus, and jealous of the honour of Persia, called the aid if divers contributary princes, and raised a mighty army, consisting of near two hundred thousand of men, which he soon shipp d in a vast navy, and landed upon the confine of Thessaly, news thereof being brought to the queen by a poor fisherman that was abroad at sea, she was in a sad distress, and committed the care of her kingdom during the absence of Dionyius, to the Lord Remus; who with the trainbands[10], and country troops, made what haste he could to their resistance, and so order'd the matter that e're they could land so vast an army, he had slain twenty thousand of them: This success encouraged him in hope for a greater victory; yet nevertheless he durst not stand battle, but made an honourable retreat toward the city, while the Persians encamp'd in the plains of Pharsalia; the next day they approached and begirt the city of Thebes on every side, laying close siege thereto, and resolved, either by famine or storm, to force them to a surrender. Olivia, Laurana, and the rest, with swoln eyes and heavy hearts, beholding the murderer of Parismus, and the authour of Dionysius's absence, as 'twere in triumph before the walls, were uttering sad complaints of their miserable estate, when behold a knight in black armour (whom therefore they termed the Black Knight (came up'n full carrier, and waving his sword thrice over his head, dared the whole army of Persia to single combat; wherein he was successful, even to admiration; for after a gallant overthrow of two Persians, horse and all, he was the third time encountred by one Bruster, a huge proportionable man, and the champion of Persia, who met the Black Knight with such violence, that they shivered their launces, and forced him to quit one of his stirrops, while Bruster himself was beaten back upon his horse's crupper. No sooner had they recovered their seats, but both drew their swords, and began a very fierce combat; which after a sharp dispute ended in conquest on the Black Knight's side; for Bruster having lost the use of his sword-arm, turned tail and fled towards the camp; which so amazed Sicanus and all the Persians, that they esteemed the Black Knight to be rather a devil than a man, seeing that after three such dangerous combats he stood unmoved, brandishing his sword and bidding defiance to Persia, On the other side, the queen and princess seeing what wonders he had done in their behalf, not knowing of whence he was, sent a page to invite him into the city, but he returned his duty and service, especially to the princess, courteously refused their invitations for reasons he might possible live to declare by word of mouth. This message being returned their wonder encreas'd, who this Black Knight should be, but guessing, could no way add to their satisfaction, since none could resolve them though they should happen to guess the right.

The next day there was news of an arrival of the King of Bohemia, King of Hungary, and Prince of Sparta, who being severally incensed with the baseness of Sicanus's treachery, came with fresh supplies to the succour of Thebes, whereupon both the Persians and the Thessalians foreseeing great slaughter like to ensue, they drew up their several armies in battalia,[11] and came to a parley, the event of which was, to decide the controversie by combat of three knights on either side, upon condition, that if the Persian knights overcame, then was Dionysius to deliver up his daughter in marriage to Sicanus, and himself become subject to the Persian crown, but if the Thessalian knights got the better, then were the Persians immediately to quit the siege, and Sicanus, upon this honour, to declare what he knew concerning the death of Parismus. These articles drawn up and agreed to on both sides, there were twenty days allowed for preparing everything in readiness against the day of combat; and in the mean time a truce made, that no acts of hostility might be offered, but such as were voluntary. During this interval, several feats of arms were performed daily at tilts and turnaments between the two armies, which afford pastime to the ladies of the courts, who took great delight in beholding the activity and success of the Black Knight; But at last it so happened that one Pollipus of the Persian forces riding up to the Black Knight, and couching[12] his launce gave him fair warning to receive him, which contrary to every bodies expectation he refused to do, but turned his horse-head about; Pollipus wandring at his refusal, resolved to know the cause; but because he would not be seen to commune with an enemy in private, he watch'd his opportunity till the evening, at which time seeing him ride out of the field, he made up to him, and desired to know the reason he refused him the same pastime he had vouchsafed other knights; Because (said he) you wear the armour of Pollipus of Phrygia, my trusy friend. In the mean time the Theban court rung with joy for the return of Dionysius, who by this time was entered with the King of Bohemia, Hungary, and Prince of Sparta, whom he there entertained most splendidly, consulting with them about erecting scaffolds, and making other preparations against the day of combat. And while they were proposing Lord Remus, Oristus, and others for combatants, a comely virgin, named Diana, arrived at the court, richly attired like a forest nymph, and bearing in her hand an escutcheon, whereon was the lively portraiture of a dying knight, wounded by slaves, and buried in a wood; being admitted into the presence, she humbly did her obeysance, and said she had a message to deliver to the Princess Laurana; who being readily called, she was presented with the escutcheon, upon which was engraven these verses:

> Since victory on virtue still attends,
> Doubt not, fair Princess, of successful friends;
> To a strange knight revenge of right belongs,
> As well for yours, as your Parismus wrongs;
> Sent by the God of Love to end the strife,
> And raise the dead Parismus unto life.

Having again and again perused the mystical lines, she knew not what construction to put upon them, or what answer readily to return; But so generously likes the offer that in civility she could do no less than accept of him her champion, though he promised such impossibilities, therefore desiring the fair messenger to return the knight unknown, her humble thanks for the tender of his service, she dismist her with a rich scarff to be presented to him, and a costly jewel for herself. Diana being gone, left the court full of joy, for the news she had brought, and of wonder who this knight should be that had so nobly undertaken the princess's quarrel with patience to expect the issue.

CHAPTER V

The dreadful battle between the six knights, wherein the Black Knight and his party claim the victory; and discovers himself to be Parismus, wonderfully preserv'd by the outlaws.

The time appointed being come, and as well the Persian as Thassalian nobles being seated upon several scaffolds, in equal expectation of success, the knights of Persia entered the lists, the first of whom was the valiant Zollus, attired all in red, and mounted upon a sorrel steed; then the two valiant brethren of Bruster, Brandor and Ramon, came galloping in so triumphant a manner, as if they had already been victorious; several times they rode about the lists, and wondred to see no enemy at hand: whereupon the Persians began to give a mighty shout, which so dismayed the Thessalians they knew not what to say, but began to think the message brought by Diana, to have been a trick put upon them by the enemy. At last, after near an hour's expectation, they beheld three knights in silver'd armour coming towards them upon a hand gallop, who soon entered the lists and declared for the Thessalians. Their apparel and plumes were all white their staves, caparisons and furniture were all alike, without the least distinction, save that one of them had on the scarf Laurana sent him, and was therefore called the princess's champion. Dionysius on the one hand descending from his chair of state, gave them thanks for their

Chap. V. *The dreadful Battle between the six Knights, wherein the Black Knight and his Party obtains the Victory; and discovers himself to be Parismus, wonderfully preserv'd by the Out-laws.*

12.   Individual combat between knights.

readiness to engage in his quarrel, and promised great tewards if it so pleased the Gods to grant them victory. The Knight with the Scarf on the other hand declaring the great delight he took in so honourable a cause, vow'd that could he be so fortunate to serve the princess Laurana, the honour gained thereby would be a greater reward then the crown of Thessaly, these ceremonies being past, and the King reinstated, the trumpets sounded a charge, and the combat began. The Knight with the Scarf encountred Zoilus, Pollipus, Brandor, and the outlaw, Ramon, amongst whom was shewn as much courage and agility as could be expected, their spears being all shivered at their first on-set, they presently drew, and dealt about such fierce and fatal blows, that in a short time the outlaw fell dead from his horse, whereat the Persians began a great shout, which they had no sooner ended, but Ramon coming to the assistance of Zoilus, had the misfortune to be run clear thro' the throat, and died immediately; Pollipus and Brandor fought a long time upon equal terms, but the Knight with the Scarf had much the advantage of Zoilus, whom summoning all his strength, he at last smote with such fury that he fell from his horse, whereupon the assembly gave so great a shout, that the earth seemed to quake, for their being two of the Thessalians left to one of the Persians, the victory was adjudged to the Thessalians.

Hereupon the King of Persia according to agreement, commanded his army immediately to withdraw; Sicanus upon his honour to declare the truth of Parismus according to the best of his knowledge: Who thereupon reply'd, By the reverence I owe to my lord and father, with the rest of the honourable assembly, I denounce him for a villain and a traytor, that does accuse me for the murder of Parismus; for by all the powers of heaven, I know nothing thereof, nor have been any way accessary thereto. In like reverence to his honourable assembly, said the Knight in the Scarf, I return that villain and traytor upon thy self, for that thou didst hire three Tartarians to murder him, who, as he was a hawking, set upon him in a wood, and in a barbarous, manner ran him in several places thro' the body, of which I myself am witness, who found him in that deplorable condi ion; all which I stand ready to justifie, and therefore as thou art a knight, and honourest arms, shew thy innocence by thy courage. Sicanus enraged hereat, seemingly accepted the challenge and withdrew to prepare himself: In the mean time the Thessalian nobles, especially the Princess Laurana, considering the wounds he had received, entreated him not to engage in a second combat: to whom he reply'd, Madam, If it be your Highness's pleasure, that the wrongs of Parismus shall go unreveng'd, I most humbly submit: but I know Madam, you are more generous, and therefore must beg your pardon. Whereupon giving him as it were her consent against her will, Sicanus (as was supposed) entered the lists, whom the wounded knight at the first on-set unhorst, having broken two of his ribs; and the company unlacing his helmet, to give him breath, found that it was not really Sicanus, but a person he had hired in his stead; which was so ill resented by the whole assembly, that they all concluded him guilty, and the King of Persia disowned him for his son, so that betwixt grief and shame in a short time after died. But the victors being carried in great triumph thro' the city, and presented with many rich gifts, at last arriving at the court, where being received with all imaginable honour, they were set down in chairs of state, the chiefest of the king's physicians being sent for to dress their wounds. Coming to take off the Knight in the Scarf's armour, it was found to be cas'd over artificially with silver, and under it black armour, so that then he was discovered to be the Black Knight, whom they thought to have been dead of his wounds in the combat with Bruster. Whereupon, Dyonisius embracing him afresh, left the uncasing of him to the King of Bohemia, as the greatest honour; which the Black Knight would by no means suffer, but humbly kneeling, desired his majesty to grant him one favour, which beimg consented to, he entreated his gracious pardon for the murderers of Parismus. But being asked why he demanded so unreasonable a demand, Because, said he, Parismus is yet in good health; upon which words he immediately discover'd himself, to the joy and wonder of all there present. And then he at large related the story of his miraculous preservation by certain outlaws, who accidentally found his wounded body in the wood, they carefully convey'd him to their cave, and chose him (after his recovery to be their general) This story seem'd at first so incredible, that they hardly durst give credit to their own eyes, but every circumstance being fully related and consider'd, they were all as it were swallowed up with wonder for a time; but at last joy prevailed, and the king would have sent for Laurana, once more to have welcomed the same person, tho' under a different character; but Parismus, the more to surprize the princes, desir'd he might be the messenger himself; to which the king easily consented, and he was conducted to her apartment; accordingly Parismus with the Lord Remus coming to the princess's lodgings, found the door fast, and imagining she might be private, stood still a while, for fear of giving her a disturbance; but after a very short pause, they heard her tune up her lute, beginning in a solemn air, and most angelical voice the following song:

> Kind knight, I know thy promise was in vain,
> To bring Parismus back to life again;
> And yet how much is to thy courage due,
> Who nobly didst the murderer subdue?
> For 'tis a part of happiness to be
> Deliver'd from misfortunes we foresee.
> All but my heart I give as a reward:
> No knight so mean a present would regard;
> It breeds, it pants, so shatter'd is and torn,
> It merits not aceptance now, but scorn;
> Yet poor Parismus shall this present have,
> Which I shall shortly carry to his grave.

So passionate were her words, and so divine her voice, that Parismus could contain himself no longer, but roundly knock'd at the door, which Leda having opened, he entred with Lord Remus; Leda shrieked, and the princess fell in a trance, absolutely imagining she had seen the ghost of Parismus. But after a long time, Lord Remus had much ado to bring her to herself, and to perswade her to the truth of what she saw, twenty times she examin'd her senses, to know if she were awake, and at last being fully convinc'd by a touch of his warm lips, that he was really, and indeed the living Parismus, 'tis impossible to say which was the greatest, her joy, or her wonder: So that half an hour's contemplation of each others happiness, the princess's in pity to his wounds, conducted him into the presence, and there openly declaring her affection to him, desiring the care of him might be committed to her charge, till he was perfectly recovered. This she did in so gallant and generous a manner, that none could tax her with the least immodesty for so doing. Insomuch that Dionysius readily granted her request, and promised to consummate her happiness in nuptial-bands, as soon as Parismus should be recover'd of his wounds, which was not long after.

CHAPTER VI

The marriage of Parismus and Laurana, how going towards Bohemia, he by treachery is left with Pollipus and Violetta (disguis'd as a page) in the Desolate Island, she carried by the tyrant Andramart to the Island of Rocks, where she is deliver'd of Parismenos, whom they threaten'd to murther if she would not admit of the tyrant's lust, but is preserved by his nurse; the enchantment of the Desolate Islands dissolv'd, &c.

And now the marriage of these two illustrious persons being solemnized with a magnificence becoming the bounty of Dionysius, and the merit of that royal pair, they spent some days in the court of Dionysius with unexpressible satisfaction, esteeming each others happiness beyond the reach even of the most adverse fortune: But, alas! the best of men and greatest of princes are equally (and perhaps more) subject to the frowns of adverse fate, than the meanest peasant: For by this time the King of Bohemia's affairs requiring his return to his own country, it was requisite that Parismus and his princess should attend him, whereupon great preparation and sorrow being made for their departure, at the time prefixt they took a kind and solemn leave of the court of Thebes, Dionysius with all his nobles attended them to the frontiers of his dominions, and returned with grief for the loss of so good company. But it must not be forgotten, that Pollipus who was resolved to accompany Parismus into Bohemia, during his residence at Thebes, chanced to be enamoured of a merchant's only daughter, named Violetta; but she out of a private kindness she bore to the prince, notwithstanding his marriage, and the impossibilty of enjoying him, resolved to seek her fortune with him in Bohemia; to which end, attiring herself in the habit of a page, she came to court, and soon got admittance into the prince's service, so that in short time they got to the port, and soon set sail for Bohemia: But the vessels being small yatchs or pleasure-boats, and their attendance numerous, it was thought fit that Parismus, Laurana, Pollipus, Leda and Violetta (now called Adonius) should go in one yatch, and the King of Bohemia, with his attendance in another: Long they had not sailed, but so fierce a tempest arose, that the ships soon lost one another, and the princes's mariners being driven to the leeward, and in danger of stranding cut their shrowds, and took off their masts by the board; but the king's mariners, whether from the skill of the seamen, or agility of the vessel, stood away to the windward, and tho' with some difficulty, made to the coast of Bohemia. Parismus and Laurana being a comfort to each other in their distress, began to think all danger blown over with the tempest, but were so deceiv'd with the approach of certain pyrates, who soon boarded them under an assurance of conquest; but by the irresistable power of Parismus, Pollipus and the rest, they met with so sharp a repulse that they were soon brought in subjection, many of them being slain, and the rest clapt under hatches: wherefore by the advice of the seamen, it was decreed to take out such goods as were of value, and with them go aboard the pyrates ship: this being done with equal courage and success, Parismus ordered some of his men to go ashore, and take in a little fresh water for fear of the worst, which accordingly they did, himself, Pollipus, and Adonius, accompanying them, a little to refresh themselves upon that pleasant shore; no sooner had the pyrates notice of this advantage they broke up the hatches, surprizing and securing the seamen Parismus had left aboard, and sinking the prince's yatch to prevent pursuit, set sail for the Island of Rocks, to which they belong'd: Parismus with the rest ashore seeing this disaster, would have done any thing to stop them in their flight; but being sensible that doing violence to himself was not a means of offering any to them, with great wisdom (I cannot say much patience) he attended the vessel with his eye, while she was within ken, and afterwards with prayers for the safety of Laurana, who poor lady, was all this while insensible of her misfortune, and only wondered at the absence of her lord. Parismus, Pollipus and Adonius, in this distress, knew not what course to take, and therefore resolv'd to stay ashore, and hale the next vessel; but the prince having spent the remaining part of the day, in a thousand complaints of his own inadvertency, blaming fortune for faults himself was guilty of, and himself for such as it was too late to repent of; at last, in the close of the evening, an aged man in mean attire came up, and courteously saluted him with his associates, as follows. Gentlemen, I perceive you are strangers brought hither by stress of weather, otherwise you would never have landed upon so dangerous a coast. Truly, father, said Parismus, you guess right; but, I pray, wherein lies the danger? Gentlemen, said he, if you will vouchsafe to accept of a poor lodging in a hermet's cell I will acquaint you more at large, where, in mean safety, you may pass away the night, which else on this shore may be hazardous. To this they thankfully consented. The poor princess all the while know not of her being prisoner, till they came to land at the Island of Rocks, where finding herself in a strange place without the comfort of her lord, she began grievously to afflict herself, but Andramart, a great tyrant, and governor of that island, having notice of this beautiful prize, came and courteously invited her into this castle, and there us'd her in a most obliging manner, hoping thereby to gain her to his lustful will, but finding fair means ineffectual, he sent his sister Adanasia who reproaching her in a most ignominious sort, torturing her with knotty whips and not allowing her, or her maid Leda necessaries for life, in such sort that she had well nigh perished, nevertheless the virtuous princes stood unmoved, and would not submit to Andramart's lust; thus for many months she lived, till at her time, it pleased the Goddess Lucina to deliver her of a son, whom she named Parismenos, and put it out to nurse. Then came the cruel Adanasia, and vow'd that unless she would yield to Andramart's love, she would murder the infant before her face. Nevertheless she committed her virtue to the care of heaven, and utterly refused to give her consent. The nurse hearing thereof, and having a tender love for so sweet a babe, fled with it into the wilderness, and there preserved it many years.

Return we now to Parismus, who by this time had understood that place to be called the Desola e Island, of which the said hermit was once king, but was supplanted by Bellona a sorceress, and driven to live in that mean estate, so having given an account at large, he desired them to accept his hard bed to refresh themselves for that night; which for a time, in civility, they refused, but with importunity at last accepted of. The climate and season being somewhat cold, they put Adonius in the middle, who poor heart! with a trembling kind of joy lay all night between her beloved Parismus, and her beloved Pollipus that little imagin'd who they had for their bed-fellow: So mean was the lodging, and so great their grief, that Parismus spent most of the night in sad complaints for the absence of his Laurana; and Pollipus for the unkindness of his Violetta; but the morning approaching they all arose, and by direction of the hermit; went towards the castle notwithstanding his earnest entreaties to the contrary. Having viewed the castle, stoutly scituated on a rock, they heard the ringing of a small bell, and in short time espied six knights in bright armour ferrying over the moat. Parismus with Pollipus, knowing they should be assaulted, received them at their landing, and with such magnanimity and success, that some fell back into the water and were drown'd, others lay dead upon the spot, and the rest submitted themselves. This news being carried to the castle, Bellona herself came out to meet them with a smiling and pleasant countenance, whom Parismus took to be some beautiful prisoner of the castle, but as he courteously addressed himself to her, she had that power with her inchantment, to cause a deep sleep to come upon them all, and commanded forthwith that they should be carried prisoners into the castle. When their senses were again restored, they were strangely surpriz'd to find themselves fast in a dungeon, and loaded with heavy irons, having no other comfort left them, but their prayers to heaven, and complaints to one another. Here they continu'd many months, under as much hardship as the cruelty of a tyrant could inflict; for Drubal, paramour to Bellona, often sent for them before him, causing them to be tortur'd in divers manners, and taking delight in their afflictions. But the enchantress seeing the resolution of Parismus and the comliness of his person, began to entertain lustful thoughts for him, which she resolved to satiate, tho' with the loss of her life. So that giving Drubal a stupefective portion, she addressed herself in an obliging manner to Parismus, causing his fetters to be taken off, and desiring him to walk with her into the garden. Parismus wondering at this strange alteration, resolved to see the event thereof, and being come into a pleasant wilderness, he soon apprehended her inclinations, and yielding a seeming compliance therewith, he at last took his opportunity, and seizing her by the hair of the head, twisted her neck in such a sort, that he set her face behind, whereof she immediately died. This being done, a strange tempest of thunder and lightning arose, which made the very earth to tremble, and the enchantment being broke, there appeared a mighty smoak about the castle, which immediately vanish'd, and left them in plain ground. After this, the place seem'd to be fill'd with fiends and damned spirits, who in a hedious sort began to torture Drubal with his servants and officers, insomuch that there was nothing to be heard but the groans and yells of damned souls, enough to have terrified the hardest knight upon earth. Nevertheless Parismus with an immoveable courage returned to find out Pollipus, Adonius, whose fetters were suddenly fallen off, and they in a strange amazement looking about them, but seeing Parismus in safety, they congratulated each others deliverance, and returned their thanks to heaven, that had so miraculously wrought the same. The rest of the prisoners likewise understanding that they owed their deliverance to Parismus, came in courteous manner and returned him thanks; amongst whom was the wife and children of Antiochus the hermit, who were by this means restored to their kingdom, which ever after they quietly enjoyed, rendring the same commodious for ships, hospitals for strangers, which some years had been ruined, desolate and avoided by mankind, as ominous and unfortunate. Antiochus in gratitude to those worthy knights, entertained them for some time courteously in his palace, and at their request hung out a flag of truce to invite ships into that port; Parismus hoping by that means, to find an opportunity of going in pursuit of his Laurana. At last, a vessel of Hungary under the command of Barzillus, put ashore, and at the request of Parismus, with a promise of great reward, stay'd there for some days, till he prepared all things in readiness for the voyage, and in solemn manner took leave of that court.

CHAPTER VII

Parismus arrives at the Island of Rocks, kills Andrimart, and with his Laurana joyfully arrives in Bohemia; Parismenos call'd the Knight of Fame, upon a vision, refuses Philaena, daughter to the King of Thrace: How he met with Angelica, daughter to the King of Natolia, was cast into the lyon's den, made his escape, found his parents fought the second time with Lord Colimus, and marrying Angelica, was crowned King of Natolia.

They had not sailed many leagues to the northward, but near the same place where they were first attacked, they were again boarded by the same pyrates, whom likewise after a fierce engagement, they once more subdued; but considering their former treachery, Parismus thought good to put the greatest part to the sword; sparing only some few to give him an account of the princess, and conduct him to the same place where she was. Whereupon one of them giving him the story at large, as has been before related, Parismus, with Pollipus and Adonius, were overjoy'd to hear of the princes's safety, and were resolved to free her from imprisonment, or dye in the attempt: This resolution the gods seemed to favour, for coming to the castle-gate, they found Andramart just alighted from hunting, with some six servants, who after a sharp dispute, Parismus with the help of Pollipus, and Barzillus, slew and subdued, and taking the keys from Andramart, who would trust none therewith in his absence, they entered the castle in triumph, surprizing and slaying the servants of Andramart at their pleasure. And now the main business was to find out the Princess Laurana, whom after a tedious and deligent search, they met with, in a room no way fitted her condition, but for its solitariness: She was leaning her head against the bosom of Leda, with wringed hands and blubber'd eyes, uttering nothing but the sweet name of her beloved Parismus. Much ado there was to make between these two (once more happy lovers) sensible of so blessed a change, but at last, fill'd with the joyful apprehensions of each others safety, they spent the time in a most refined and spotless enjoyment of each other. By this time Parismus having understood the cruel usage Laurana met with, and the supposed murder of Parismenos, he reveng'd himself by the death of the cruel Adamasia, the author thereof, and returned into his own country; but with what joy these long absent princes were received in the Bohemian court, no pen is able to express, nor any reader sufficiently to comprehend. Violetta, who in all their travels had been their bed-fellow, and was an eye and ear witness to the sincerity of Pollipus his love, began to consider how imprudent, and little less than dishonourable her passion for Parismus would appear, she began to harbour kind thoughts of her lover, and finding it no time to dally, for that he was now taking his leave of Parismus to go in quest after her, she discovered herself to his unspeakable joy, and was in a short time married to him, with the greatest pomp and solemnity that court could afford.

Parismenos by time grown to some years, began to think himself born to greater matters than always to live in a wood, and tho' his nurse could give him no account of his parentage, he found in himself a prince-like mind, fitted for great atchievmnts;[13] while he thought of these things, and was rambling up and down with his nurse, resolving to seek his fortune, a lyon met them, and immediately seizing the nurse, slew her, but turning towards Parismus wagg'd his tail and fawned upon him, insomuch that the harmless youth, was very proud of his new companion, made much of him, and went with him that night to his den;[14] but as he slept in the bosom of his bed-fellow, his nurse seemed to appear to him, willing him to go to the castle of Andramart, by which means he should know his parentage, and become a great prince. Being awake in the morning, he considered of his dream but knew not what the castle of Andramart should mean; however he resolved to go out of those woods, and view the country; and accordingly seeing a castle upon a high hill at a distance, he bent his course that way, and before noon arriv'd there. The inhabitants of the castle, tho' now in subjection to Parismus could not leave off their old trade of pyrating, and seeing this strange youth, they took him abroad, in hopes of making some traffick with him, but meeting with a vessel of Barbary commanded by one Igridam, they met with so sharp a repulse, that it had not been for the valour of Parismenos, they had certainly been taken; while this dispute lasted, there arose a mighty tempest, which separated the combatants and so shatter'd the pyrates ship, that she foundred in the sea, but Parismenos by good fortune getting astride a piece of the main-mast; was driven ashore upon the coast of Thrace: Where being courteously entertained by Duke Amalenus, he performed such acts of chivalry, that he was stiled the Knight of Fame. During his stay in those parts, the King of Thrace ordained a general triumph to be held for certain days upon the account of his fair and only daughter Philena, to whom many knights pretended affection, and win the prize, should marry his daughter. After several brave atchievements by divers valiant knights, it was Parismenos's luck to win the prize: But having understood that Philena had already given her heart to one Remulry, a knight of Thrace, he very generously quitted his right in her, and left her to her own disposal. The same evening the Goddess of Love appeared to him in a vision leading in her hand a most beautiful virgin, whom when Parismenos had greedily viewed, attempting to grasp her, the Goddess thus replied:

> Sir Knight of Fame, of kingly race begot,
> This Lady for thy Princess I alot;
> Whose name in Libian or Natolian Land,
> Thou with long search at last shall understand:
> But e're that day you'll meet with great distress,
> And prove that grief's the way to happiness.

Parismenos having duly considered her words, and bearing the perfect idea of the beautiful lady in his mind, he soon perceived she had not the least resemblance of Philena; and therefore being highly satisfied with what he had done, he in short time departed towards the country of Natolia, being nearer to that part of Thrace, that the country of Lybia.

Many days had the Knight of Fame travelled without any adventure, till arriving in a pleasant valley he alighted from his steed by reason of the heat, and under the shade of a spreading scicamore, laid his weary limbs to repose, when the fair Angelica, daughter of Maximus, King of Natolia, (having that day forsaken the Golden Tower to meet her father) passed by, and spying Parismenos, supposing he had been dead, sent one of her knights to see who he was; who being suddenly awakened, no sooner beheld the divine Angelica, but his fancy so suggested her to be the same whom he had seen in the vision; so that mounting, and having satisfied her curiosity with a civil, but common reply, he mixt himself with her train: The princess soon after dropping her glove, the Knight of Fame, nimbler than any of her retinue, flung himself from his horse, and with due reverence, and most sweet and charming grace, presented it to her highness, who freely gave it to him for his pains. This favour being envied by the Lord Collimus, one of her great knight, he rudely commanded him to surrender it; but instead of compliance found a repulse, being overthrown to the ground in the sight of Angelica and the king her father, who just at that instant entred the valley, and understanding the cause of their encounter, blam'd Collimus's rashness, as much as the stranger's prowess, and having receiv'd what satisfaction he could of the Knight of Fame's quality, graciously invited him to the court. Here he got an opportunity to offer his vows to Angelica, who soon beheld him with gracious eyes; an attemp of no small danger, for by teason of an old prophesie, that her marriage should be the occasion of her father's death, the king strictly guarded her in the Golden Tower from all addresses of that kind; and being advertised by some court-ear-wiggs of their amorous correspondence, in a jealous fury imprisoned his lovely daughter, and cast the Knight of Fame (upon a feigned pretence of treason) into the lion's den, which according to the natural instinct of those noble beasts, refusing to offer the least violence to such a royal prey, he continued divers days in miserable condition, feeding upon the

13.   A storm at sea.

garbidge and offel thrown into the den, till the keeper coming to clean it, whilst he stood amazed to find him alive, the Knight of Fame snatch'd his dagger from him, and made him swear to conceal his escape; in which auspicious fortune directed his uncertain flight towards the country of Bohemia, upon whose confines he was scarce arrived, when he heard the dismal shrieks of a lady whom an insolent villain was about to ravish; the brave Parismenos not us'd to trifle time in d scou se[29] upon such occasions, immediately made at him with his sword, and after an obstinate fight, left him dead upon the spot: Then turning to the lady, and having received her compliments of gratitude, she requested him to conduct her to the Bohemian court, for in truth she was no other than the before mentioned Violetta, who walking a little way from the palace had been surprized by a barbarous out-law nam'd Archas from whose lust the gallant knight had thus happily rescued her.

At the Bohemian court, upon Violetta's relation of his bravery, the Knight of Fame was sumptuously received; both Parismus and Laurana (who had oft heard of his renown) at first contracting a strange kindness, or rather passionate fondness towards him, especially the queen, who some time after, desiring an account of his adventures, he told her how his birth was unknown, but brought up in the Isle of Rocks, that his nurse was slain by a lion, and most other accidents, adding, that he was confidently assured by his Genius, that he was of royal race, but had no other evidence to clear his descent but a jewel, which his nurse had charged him to keep. Laurana, who felt unusual transports in her breast all the while he was speaking, no sooner saw the jewel, but she remembred it, and at the same instant clasping her arms about his neck, welcom'd him as her son Parismenos, whom she supposed to have slain by the tyrant Andramart. Nor was Parismus less satisfied, his age features, and other circumstances so agreeing. This discovery filled the whole court with joy and triumphs, only Parismus still wore clouds upon his face, and a deeper sorrow on his heart, both for the absence of Angelica, and the deplorable state he left her in; which being taken notice of by his parents, he at last recounted to them the whole story of the mutual passion they had for each other, and the cruelty the King of Natolia had used to him, who still knew nor (suspected) no less but that he was long since devoured by the lyons.

Upon this ambassadors was dispatch'd to the Notolian[30] court by Parismus complaining of the out-rage, and threatning vengeance for the unjust death of his son; who being answered by Maximus with slights and affronts, Parismus and his Parismenos, with a flying army enter'd his terrotories, but with a greater shew of bravery than hostility, not doing the least injury to any of his subjects; however, Maximus to drive them out, raises a mighty force, and both armies being in view of each other, after several skirmishes, at the intreaty of Parismenos, who still conceal'd his being alive from the enemy, his father offered to decide the justice of his arms by single combat; which being accepted of, Parismenos was the challenger on the Bohemian party; and the Lord Collimus, (a man always of an enterprizing haughty spirit) undertook to answer him; but victory entail'd on the sword of Parismenos, rendered him conqueror. Whereupon an interview being laid between the kings, and a declaration of the young prince's prodigious escape; the Lady Angelica was by him demanded in marriage; which in such a juncture, his Natolian Majesty, tho' not willing to grant, yet knew not how to deny; so that being sent for into the field, the two happy lovers were there contracted to their unspeakable satisfaction. But in vain do poor mortals endeavour to avoid the decrees of Fate; for in the tilts and turnaments perform'd in honour of the nuptials, by the fall of in over-crowded scaffold, divers people, and particularly King Maximus was kill'd. This disaster put a present damp upon those splendid solemnities, till time and better consideration had rendred the mourners obedient to the unavoidable laws of destiny, and then Parismenos having married the undoubted heiress of Natolia, was joyfully received and crowned king of that potent country; and having setled affairs and magnificently treated his father, at last was forced to take leave of him, who with honour and full satisfaction returned with his troops to his own dominions; leaving Parismenos possest of a mighty crown, and the far more valuable society of his dear Angelica; between whom there were begot a race of heroes, whose renowned actions shall in future ages deserve larger history than this, to which our weary pen unwilling subscribes an end.

FINIS

14. A banquet with, apparently, a stag hunt passing through.

The diners are in late seventeenth-century costume which is consistent with
the lack of concern for accurate periodisation throughout the illustrations to
this chapbook.

Valentine and Orson

THE FAMOUS
HISTORY
OF
VALENTINE & ORSON,
The Two SONS of the
EMPEROR OF GREECE.

Reader, you'll find this little Book contains
Enough to anſwer thy Expence and Pains.

London: Printed for, and Sold by C. SHEPPARD,
No. 8, Aylesbury Street, Clerkenwell.
[Price One Penny.]
1804.

Mary Rhynd, Printer, 21, Ray Street, Clerkenwell.

15. The title page of *Valentine and Orson.*

The title page of *Valentine and Orson* showing printing details and a cut of a
knight. This is a stock item: *Valentine and Orson* chapbooks commonly show
a scene from the story.

THE FAMOUS

HISTORY

OF

VALENTINE AND ORSON

The Two SONS of the

EMPEROR OF GREECE

Reader, you'll find this little Book contains
Enough to answer thy Expence and Pains[1]

LONDON: PRINTED for and sold by C. SHEPPARD,
No. 8, Aylesbury Street,
Clerkenwell.

[Price One Penny] 1804

Mary Rhynd, Printer,
21, Ray Street, Clerkenwell

The History of Valentine and Orson

CHAPTER I

In which the reader his informed how Lady Bellisant is delivered of Valentine and Orson, at one Birth, in a Wood.

History tells us that Pepin, King of France, had a fair sister named Bellisant, who was married to Alexander, the Emperor of Greece, and by him carried to his capital at Constantinople; from whence, after having lived with great virtue, she was banished through the means of a false accuser, whom she had severely checked for his imprudence[2]; and though at that time she was big with child, yet she was compelled to leave her husband's empire, to the great regret of the people, attended only with a squire named Blandiman.

After great fatigue and travel, she arrived in the forest of Orleans, where, finding her pains come thick upon her, she dismissed her attendant for a midwife, but before his return, was delivered of two lovely children, one of which was conveyed away by a she bear, which she pursued on her hands and knees, leaving the other behind.[3] But before her return, King Pepin, being a hunting in the forest, came to the tree where she had left the other babe, and causing it to be taken up, sent it to nurse, and when it grew up, he called its name Valentine. Blandiman at length came back, and instead of finding his mistress found her brother Pepin at the tree to whom he declared all that had happened; and how his sister was banished through the false suggestions of the arch priest; which when King Pepin heard, he was greatly enraged against the

22

him to hell, to fee his falfe prophet Mahomet.

The Pagans feeing their King dead, threw down their arms and ran, and the Chriftians purfued them with a mighty flaughter. At laft the purfuit being over, they returned to Conftantinople, and Orfon acquainted the Emprefs of the death of his father, but concealed by whom it was done.

Upon which it was concluded that Valentine and Orfon fhould govern the empire by turns, with their wives, the Ladies Fazon and Clerimond, whofe brother, the Green Knight, was crowned King of the Green Mountain, the people of which were much delighted to have fo brave a warrior for their King.

THE

HISTORY

OF

Valentine and Orson.

CHAP. I.

In which the reader his informed how Lady Bellisant is delivered of Valentine and Orson, at one Birth, in a Wood.

HISTORY tells us that Pepin, King of France, had a fair fifter, named Bellifant, who was married to Alexander, the Emperor of Greece, and by him carried to his capital at Conftantinople; from whence, after having lived with great virtue, fhe was banifhed through the means of a falfe accufer, whom fhe had feverely checked for his imprudence; and though at that time

A 2

16. The first and last pages of *Valentine and Orson.*

The first and last pages of the chapbook showing vignettes drawn from the printer's stock and having no particular relationship to the text. The image of children dancing on page one reminds us both of the important part that children played in forming the audience for this type of text and of the debt to chapbooks in the work of William Blake. The closing vignette is purely decorative.

Lady Bellisant, saying, that the emperor ought to have put her to death. So leaving Blandiman, he returned with his nobles to Paris.[4]

The Lady Bellisant having followed the bear to no purpose, returned to the place where she had left the other babe; but great was her sorrow when Blandiman said, he had seen her brother Pepin, but could tell nothing of the child, and having comforted her for the loss of it, they went to the sea side, took shipping, and arrived at the castle of the great[5] Feragus, in Portugal.

All this while the bear nourished the infant among her young ones, until at length it grew up a wild hairy man, doing great mischief to all that passed through the forest; in which we will leave him, and return to the arch priest, who did great mischief, until he was impeached by a merchant, of having wrongfully accused the empress; upon which they fought, and the merchant conquering, made the priest confess all his treasons. The emperor wrote about it to the King of France, and he was hanged.

CHAPTER II

Valentine conquers his brother orson in the forest of orleans.

Now was Valentine grown a lusty young man, and by the king was greatly beloved, as if he had been his own child; commanding him to be taught the use of arms, in which he soon became so expert, that few in the court dared to encounter him; which made Hufray and Henry, the king's bastard sons exceedingly envy him. At this juncture great complaints were made against the wild man, from whom no knight had escaped with his life that had encountered him, which made the king promise a thousand marks to any one that should bring him dead or alive, which offer none dare accept; but Hufray and Henry desired King Pepin to send Valentine, with a view of getting rid of so powerful a rival in the king's favour, but his majesty seeing their malice, was very angry, telling them he had rather lose the best baron in the land.

However, Valentine desired leave of his majesty to go to the forest, resolving either to conquer the wild man, or die in the attempt. Accordingly, having furnished himself with a good horse, and arms, he set forward on his journey, and after hard travelling he arrived in the forest; in the evening he tied his horse to a large spreading oak; and got up in a tree himself, for his security, where he rested that night.

Next morning he beheld the wild man traversing the forest in search of his prey; at length he came to the tree where Valentine's horse stood, from whom he pulled many hairs, upon which the horse kicked him. The wild man feeling the pain was going to tear him to pieces, which Valentine seeing, made signs as if he would fight him, and accordingly he stepped down and gave him a blow, but the wild man caught him by the arm and threw him to the ground, then taking up Valentine's shield, he beheld it with amaze, in respect to the colours thereon emblazoned.

Valentine being much bruised, got up and came to his brother in much anger; but Orson ran to a tree, and then they engaged; but both being terribly wounded, gave out by consent; after which Valentine signified to Orson, that if he would yield to him, he would order matters so as he would become a rational creature.

Orson thinking that he meant him no harm, stretched forth his hands to him; upon which he bound him, and then led him to Paris, where he presented him to King Pepin, who had the wild man baptised by the name of Orson, from his being taken in a wood.[6] Orson's actions during their stay there very much amused the whole court[7]: at length the Duke of Acquitian[8] sent letters, importing, that whoever should overcome the Green Knight, a fierce pagan champion, should have his daughter Fazon in marriage. Upon which proposition Valentine set out for that province, attended by his brother Orson, by which means he came to the knowledge of his parents, as we shall find hereafter.

CHAPTER III

The fight between orson & the green knight

AFTER a long journey, Valentine and Orson arrived at Duke Savory's palace in Acquitain, - and making known the reasons that

17. A tournament.

Compare illustration 3. Cuts of this kind are found throughout a whole range of chapbooks and could be drawn from the printer's stock to serve a number of purposes.

they came there, were presented to Fazon, to whom Valentine thus addressed himself.

"Sweet creature! King Pepin has sent me hither with the bravest knight in all his realm, to fight the Green Knight, who, tho' he is dumb and naked, is endued with such valour, that no knight under the sun is able to cope with him." During this speech she viewed Orson narrowly, and he her; but supper coming in, interrupted them, and they sat down to eat.

Whilst they were in the midst of all their feasting, the Green Knight entered, saying, Noble Duke of Acquitain, hast thou any more knights to cope with me for thy daughter? Yes, replied the Duke, I have seventeen, and then shewed them to him.

The Green Knight then said to them, Eat your fill, for tomorrow will be your last.

Orson hearing what he said, was much incensed against him, and suddenly rising from the table, threw the Green Knight with such force against the wall as laid him dead for some time; which much pleased the whole company.

Next day many knights went to fight the Green Knight, but he overcame and slew then all, until at last, Orson, being armed in Valentine's armour, came to the Green Knight's pavilion, and defying him, they began the most desperate combat that was ever heard of, and the Green Knight made so great a stroke at him, as cut off the top of his helmet, and half his shield, wounding him very much.

But this served only to enrage the valiant Orson, who coming to him on foot took hold of him, and pulling him from his horse, got astride him, and was just going to kill him, but was prevented by Valentine, who interceded with Orson to spare his life, on condition of his turning Christian, and acquainted King Pepin how he was conquered.

The Green Knight having promised to perform all that was desired, they led him prisoner to the city of Acquitain; and the Duke received them with great joy, and offered the Lady Fazon to Orson; but he would not marry her till his brother had won the Green Knight's sister, Lady Clerimond; nor till they had talked

18. A knight blowing a horn outside a castle.

   This is not, in fact, an incident from the text and relates more closely to an
   episode in *The Seven Champions of Christendom*, though in romance
   narrative there are several examples of this action.

with the enchanted head of brass to know his parents, and get the proper use of his tongue.[9]

Which, when the lady knew, she was sorrowful, because she loved Orson, and resolved to marry none but him, who had so nobly conquered the Green Knight.

CHAPTER IV

Valentine and orson going in search of lady clerimond, who had the brazen head in her possession.

VALENTINE and Orson having taken leave of the Duke of Acquitain, and his daughter Fazon, proceeded on their journey in search of the Lady Clerimond, and at last came to a tower of burnished brass; which upon enquiry, they discovered to be kept by Clerimond, sister to Feragus and the conquered Green Knight, and asking entrance, were refused it by the centinel, which provoked Valentine to that degree, that he run against him with such fury, that the centinel fell down dead immediately.

The Lady Clerimond beheld all this dispute, and seeing them brave knights received them courteously. Valentine having presented tokens from the Green Knight, told her he came there for love of her, and to discourse with the all-knowing head, concerning their parents.

After dinner the Lady Clerimond took them by the hand, and led them to the chamber of varieties, where the head was placed between four pillars of pure jasper; when they entered, it made the following speeching to Valentine.

"Thou famous knight of royal extract, art called Valentine the Valiant, who of right ought to marry the Lady Clerimond. Thou art son to the Emperor of Greece, and the Empress Bellisant, who is now in the Castle of Feragus in Portugal, where she has resided for 20 years. King Pepin is thy uncle, and the wild man thy brother; the Empress Bellisant brought ye two forth in the forest of Orleans: he was taken away by a revenous bear, and thou wast taken up by thine uncle Pepin, who brought thee up to man's estate. Moreover,

I likewise tell thee that thy brother shall never speak until thou cuttest the thread that groweth under his tongue."

The brazen head having ended his speech, Valentine embraced Orson, and cut the thread that grew under his tongue; and he directly related many surprising things.

After which Valentine married Lady Clerimond, but not before she had turned a Christian.

In this castle there lived a dwarf, named Pacolet, who was an enchanter, and by his art had contrived a horse of wood, and in the forehead a fixed pin, by turning of which he could convey himself to the farthest part of the world.[10]

This enchanter flies to Portugal and informed Feragus of his sister's nuptials, and of her turning Christian; which so enraged him that he swore by Mahomet he would make her rue it; and therefore got ready his fleet and sailed towards the castle of Clerimond, where, when he arrived, he concealed his malice from his sister, and also the two knights, telling them that he came to fetch them into Portugal, the better to solemnize their marriage, and he would turn Christian on their arrival at his castle all which they believed, and soon after embarked with him.

When he had got them on board, he ordered them to be put in irons, which so much grieved his sister Clerimond, that she would have thrown herself into the sea, had she not been stopped.

CHAPTER V

Pacolet comforts the ladies and delivers valentine and orson out of prison

WHEN they were come to Portugal, he put Valentine and Orson into a dungeon, and fed them with bread and water, but allowed his sister Clerimond the liberty of the castle, where she met the Empress Bellisant, who had been confined 20 years in the castle of Feragus.

She seeing her so full of grief comforted her, enquiring the reason, which she told her.

The empress was mightily grieved, but Pacolet comforted them, telling them he would release them all that evening, the which he accordingly did in the following manner. In the dead of night he goes to the dungeon, where lay Valentine and Orson, bound in chains, and touching the doors with his magic wand, they flew open; and coming to the knights, he released them and conducted them to the apartment where Bellisant and Clerimond were, who were exceedingly transported; but Pacolet hindered them from discoursing long, by telling them they must depart before the guards of Feragus awaked, which would put a stop to his proceedings. So Pacolet led them out of the castle, and having prepared a ship, he conveyed them to Lady Fazon, at the city of Acquitain. Next morning when Feragus heard of their escape, he was enraged to the last degree.

The knights and ladies being out of danger, soon arrived at Acquitain, to the great joy of Lady Fazon, who was soon after married with Orson with great solemnity; upon which tilts and tournaments were performed for many days; but Valentine carried the prize, overthrowing at least an hundred brave knights.

CHAPTER VI

Feragus raises a mighty army, and lays siege to the city of acquitain.

FERAGUS, to be revenged on them, assembled an army, marched against the city of Acquitain, and laid close siege to it, with a vast army of Saracens; when Duke Savery perceived it, he resolved to give them battle the very next morning, and accordingly he sallied forth with all his forces, but venturing too far, he was taken by the Saracens, and carried to Feragus's tent.

Now Orson was resolved to set him free, or lose his life; so putting on the armour of a dead Saracen, he called Pacolet, and went through the enemy without being molested, until they arrived at the tent where the Duke was confined; which done, they gave him a horse, and shewed him the road to the Christian army; on their return a general shout was made by all the army. "Long live the Duke of Acquitain!" which so dismayed the Saracens, that they fled away in confusion, and the Christians pursued them, till the night obliged them to give over.

Soon after the victory, Valentine, Orson, the Ladies Bellisant, Clerimond and Fazon, set out for Constantinope, to see the emperor their father, after they had taken leave of Duke Savary and his nobles, and were received with great joy.

At length the emperor set out from Constantinople after taking leave of his family, to visit a strong castle he had in Spain.

While he was absent, Brandiser, brother to Feragus invaded the empire with a very great army, and at length besieged Constantinople, where lay Valentine and Orson, the Green Knight, and all the ladies.

Valentine seeing the condition they were all in, resolved to give Brandiser battle, and thereupon divided his army into ten battalions, commanded by ten knights, and sallying out of the city, began the fight with the Saracens, who drew up in readiness to receive them.

In the meantime the emperor, who was at sea, met a fleet going to the assistance of Brandiser, which bore upon him with full sails; whereupon exhorting his companions to behave like men, they made ready to receive them, and after a most bloody and obstinate battle, the emperor got the victory, having slain many of the pagans, and dispersed their ships.

After this victory, the emperor commanded his men to put on the arms of the vanquished, as he did himself, thinking thereby the better to fall upon the besiegers; but the stratagem proved most fatal to him, as we shall hereafter find.

All this while the Christians and Valentine bravely encountered Brandiser and his men before the walls of Constantinople, sometimes getting and sometimes losing ground: but at length Valentine came to the standard of Brandiser, where an Indian king ran against him with great force, but Valentine avoiding him, struck him with such fury as cleft him down the middle.

On the other hand, Orson and the Green Knight were not idle, but with their brandished swords cut themselves a passage quite through the pagan army, destroying all that opposed them.

Soon after news came that a mighty fleet of Saracens were entering the harbour; whereupon Valentine judged it was necessary to go thither, and oppose their landing, but it proved fatal; for in this fleet was the emperor his father, who being clad in Saracens armour, Valentine by mistake ran him quite through the body with his spear; which when he knew, he was going to kill himself; had not his brother and the Green Knight prevented him; but getting a horse with an intent to lose his life, he rushed in the midst of the enemy, till he came to the giant Brandiser, who, when he saw Valentine, encountered him so fiercely, that both fell to the ground; but Valentine recovering, gave him a stab, which sent him to hell, to see his false prophet Mahomet.

The pagans seeing their king dead, threw down their arms and ran, and the Christians pursued them with a mighty slaughter. At last the pursuit being over, they returned to Constantinople, and Orson acquainted the empress of the death of his father, but concealed by whom it was done.

Upon which it was concluded, that Valentine and Orson should govern the empire by turns, with their wives, the ladies Fazon and Clerimond, whose brother, the Green Knight, was crowned King of the Green Mountain; the people of which were much delighted to have so brave a warrior for their king.

CHAPTER VII

Valentine dies, and orson turns hermit

NOW Valentine being greatly vexed in mind for the death of his father, who he killed out of a mistake, resolved to make a pilgrimage to the Holy Sepulchre: and taking leave of his wife Clerimond, and giving the government of the empire unto his brother, he departed to the great sorrow of all, particularly his brother Orson and the fair Clerimond.[11]

Valentine, after seven years absence, returned, dressed like a poor palmer, begging victuals at the gate of his own palace: and at length being sick, and about to die, he called for Clerimond, and made himself known to her, at which she was ready to give up the ghost.[12]

At least having recommended the care of her to his brother, and the empress his dear mother, and asking a blessing of them, he turned on one side and breathed out his noble soul from his illustrious body, to the great grief of all the valiant knights of Christendom, to whom he had been a noble example, and a generous reliever. But Clerimond never would espouse any one, but betook her to a single life, always lamenting the loss of her beloved husband.

After his death, Orson governed the empire with great wisdom and justice for seven years, till at length, seeing the fragile state of human affairs, he gave the charge of his empire, wife and children, to the Green Knight, and then turning hermit, he became once more a voluntary resident of the forests and woods, where, after living to a great age, this magnamious and invincible hero surrendered up his body unto never sparing death.[13]

> Thus, reader, you may see that none withstand
> Tho' great in valour, or in vast command
> The mighty force of death's all conquering hand.

FINIS

The Seven Wise Masters
of Rome

THE

HISTORY

OF THE

Seven Wise Masters

of

Rome

CONTAINING
Many excellent and delightful Examples, with their Explatations[1]
and modern
Significations, which (by way of allu
sion) may be termed, An Historicall
comparison of Sacred and Civil Trans
actions; the better to make an im
pression on the minds of Men.

FALKIRK:
Printed by T Johnston.
1816

The History of the Seven Wise Masters

CHAPTER I

There reigned in the city of Rome a famous emperor, whose wife excelled in virtue all the rest of her sex; he had by this wife one son, named Dioclesian. The emperor assembled his nobles to advise how he might train up his son. Their opinion was that he should send for the Seven Wise Masters. The young prince thus disposed of, his mother, the queen, soon after died, and the emperor having lived single for some time, the Roman lords besought him to take a second wife. At this all the courts of Europe were searched for an accomplished lady. At length they pitched on the King of Castile's daughter, of whom the emperor much approved. The marriage being concluded, she came to Rome, and there, with great pomp, the nuptials were celebrated - The young empress, having no child, studied how she might destroy the young prince; and the better to do it, prevailed with her lord to send for him to court, But the hasty and unexpected message caused the masters to suspect some evil: they consulted the planets, and found, that if the prince went at that time, and spoke at all, he would die a violent death; and yet, if he went not, they would lose their heads, which they would rather do than hazard his life. Whilst they were in this anxiety, the prince came down and demanded the cause of their troubles? The which they related, with their resolution. With that he viewed the firmament, and found the constellations more propitious, for it now appeared, that if he abstained from speaking seven days, he would escape the death threatened; desiring his masters to intercede in his favour, and make an apology to the emperor for his not speaking for such a time; and withal he told them a dream that he had dreamed, viz. That his bed-chamber seemed to be turned up side-down. From which they presaged good success, promising to do their utmost for his preservation; and thereupon set him upon a stately horse, clothed in purple and gold, and attended him to his father's court. The emperor came forth and embraced him; enquiring for his welfare; the which the prince gave no answer; whereat the emperor marvelled! yet, supposing it was so ordered by the masters, he conducted him to the palace, and seated him next the throne; interrogating many things; but he answered none. While the emperor's thoughts were taken up in wondering at his son's silence, The empress came in, adorned with costly robes; and understanding which was her son-in-law, received him with becoming kindness; and taking him aside, by emperor's consent she undertook to make him speak.

> Tho' with intens[2] his virtue to betray,
> That to his life she might make easy way.

CHAPTER II

The Empress' wicked scheme

The empress, fired with the beauty of the young prince, sought many a means to entice him to a rich alcove, telling him that she would die, and leave her royalty, if he denied her love. This he refused, tho' in silence. Whereupon she brought him pen, ink, and paper, desiring him to write a reply; which he did to this effect: "Madam, the laws of my Creator forbid so great wickedness, as to defile my father's bed. Fatal Madam, would be the consequence, both from avenging heaven, and my father's wrath; therefore, on my knees, I implore you would proceed no farther." Hereupon he fell on his knees. The empress seeing this, turned her love to hatred, tearing her face and robes in a most wretched manner, crying out for help. At this alarm, the emperor came and demanded the cause? When she declared, that the prince would have been rude with her, and forced her to lewdness. The emperor then commanded that he should be put to death directly. Upon which the nobles fell on their knees before their lord, and begged a respite for his execution to which the emperor agreed: - Which pleased all but the empress.

CHAPTER III

PANTILLUS, the first Master's Intercession

The empress, grieving at the delay of the son's execution, told the emperor the following example, saying, If this son lived, it would fare with him as with a Roman nobleman, who had in his orchard a fair tree bearing fruit; but one day he saw springing from the root thereof, a young scion; at which he rejoiced, saying, That that would be a fair tree. But finding that it encreased not in growth, he asked at the gardener the reason? Who answered that the large branches of the old tree kept the sun and falling showers from it. Whereupon he caused many to be cut off. Yet finding the body of the old tree impaired the nourishment of the young scion, he caused it to be hewn down; which being done, the young scion withered. Even so, said she, is your case; you are the tree, and your son the scion, that is inciting your subjects to rise against your life, that he may reign. That shall not be, said the emperor, for to-morrow he shall surely die.

The day appointed being come, the prince was delivered unto the executioner. Which Pantillus, the first master, hearing, he hasted to the palace, and told the emperor the following example.

There once lived a knight in this city who had a son, whom leaving to the care of some nurses, he often went abroad, delighting in hawking and hunting, and among his dogs he had a grey-hound. One day going to a tournament he left his hound and falcon at home; at which time, the cradle, in which the son was, was standing in the hall, the nurses absent from it, and the grey-hound sleeping by it; the falcon espied a serpent creeping out of a hole in the wall; going towards the child: upon which, shaking and fluttering his bells, he awaked the grey-hound, who killed the serpent and saved the child; yet, in the bustle, the cradle was overturned, and the child was whelmed under it, the grey-hound lying down by it, and licking its wounds; which the servants seeing, ran and told the lady the news, who with them concluded the hound had devoured his son; whereupon the father struck off the hound's head; but afterwards found his mistake.[3] So, said the master, it will happen unto you. - Then said the emperor, he shall not die.

CHAPTER IV

LENTULLUS, the second master's Intercession.

The empress hearing that the master had prevailed with the emperor, came and besought him, that his son might be put to death, lest it should happen to him, as to a wild boar, thus: There was a mighty emperor, whose empire was wasted by a boar, which obliged the emperor to proclaim, That whosoever killed him, should have his daughter in marriage, and after his decease, the empire. Many attempted, but in vain, until a shepherd, with only a staff, resolved to venture on him; but, beholding his tusks, etc. was afraid to touch him; therefore betook to a tree, on which grew delicious fruit; but the boar shaking it so, he was fearful of its falling; therefore he threw down the fruit thereof, which so satisfied him, that he lay down to sleep: In the interim, the shepherd descended, and struck the beast to the heart; and so won what the emperor had promised. Consider then, my lord, the case in yours: you are the mighty boar, against which open force cannot prevail, but secret fraud may deprive you of your life and empire, whilst you hearken to the masters. -

Then said the emperor he shall die.

The second master, named Lentullus, on hearing that the empress had again prevailed, came before the emperor, entreating him to spare his son's life, lest it happen him as it did to a Roman knight, that espoused a beautiful wife, and fearing she would stray, locked the doors evry night, laying the key under his head; but she stole in from thence, and went and sported with her gallants. But one night missing her, he bolted the door: she returned and knocked, but he upbraided her for her inconstancy saying, she should stay till the watch seized her. - Whereupon she took two large stones, and threw them into a well that was in the court-yard, then hid herself under the door. At which the knight, thinking she had jumped into the well, came down to relieve her; when, upon his opening the door, she slipped in, and bolted him out, calling for the watch to seize him; who adjudged him to stand in the pillory.[4] - This story so much moved the emperor, That, says he, this day my son shall not die.

CHAPTER V

CRATOA, the third Master's intercession

The empress being exceeding outrageous, and the emperor finding nothing would divert her fury, promised her his death once more. There lived, said she, a knight at Rome, who spent great riches, and was reduced to poverty, so that he was about to sell his inheritance; but his son and two daughters urged the contrary: Whereupon he, resolved with his son to break into the emperor's treasury. He did so, and took thence as much gold as both could carry. They attempted it again a second time; the father went first and was caught in a trap: whereupon he desired the son to strike off his head, lest, being discovered, his family should die. The son accordingly complied, and bore away the head; but the next morning the body being found, was, by the emperor's order, dragged about the city, with command, that wherever they heard any weeping, as the body passed by, to enter that house, and convey those therein to the gallows, for of that house was he lord: when the body came near the knight's house, the daughter shrieked, when to prevent the discovery, the son wounded himself; and insinuated that that was the cause. The officers were satisfied, and carried the body to the place of execution, and hanged it up; yet the son would neither take it down, nor bury the dead, tho' the father died to save his life. - Even so, said she, is your case by your son, who seeks your life and my honour. That shall not be, for to-morrow he shall die, said the emperor.

When she had told her story, Cratoa, the third master, came in, saying, Dread Sovereign, if your son die, it shall happen to you as with a knight, who killed a pye, that he exceedingly loved, thus: A knight married a wife, who took to unlawful pleasures; which being perceived by the pye, whom the knight had taught most languages, he told his master what had happened in his absence; for which the lady hated him: and to prevent it for the future, she untiled the house, and cast down sand, stones and water upon him; which the pye took for hail, rain and snow. So when his lord came home, he told he was almost killed by reason of the heavy tempest which fell upon him. The wife hearing him say so, answered, My lord, you may now see the error in crediting this bird, for there has not been a fairer day in the memory of man. The knight upon this inquired of his neighbours, who confirmed what she said. He therefore broke the neck of the pye, but after the deed, he saw the house untiled with the gravel, etc. lying on the top of the house, which persuaded him the pye had been deceived. - Deceived indeed, said the emperor; and, for the example's sake, my son shall not die this day.

The empress hearing this, answered, My lord, in this city reigned an emperor, named Tiberius, who had seven counsellors, who being skilful in magic, so ordered by their charms, that the emperor's eyes had had a continual mist before them; but the empress, sitting at the table with her lord, comforted him the best way, desiring to command his chief counsellors, on pain of death, to restore him to sight. The emperor then sent for the magic counsellors, and charged them to tell the reason of his blindness, and find a cure. After long puzzling, they found a youth, who interpreted a dream of a spring, which rising small, soon overflowed the ground: and the man accordingly, digging, found great treasure, as the youth had interpreted. They desired him to go with them, and he would be rewarded. - Coming before the emperor, he desired to be let into the royal bed-chamber, where, casting off the bed-clothes, there appeared a seeming well, fed with seven springs, which the youth said must be stopped ere he could have his sight in another place. Then he demanded of him, How must they be stopped? To which the youth answered, The seven springs signified his seven counsellors, who had usurped his royal authority, casting a mist of delusion before his eyes, that he might not behold their extortion. Therefore strike off their heads, said he, and the springs shall cease. To this he consented; the springs vanished, and his sight was restored. - Just so, said she, is it with you and your seven masters. On this he again consented that his son should die.

CHAPTER VI

MALQUIDRAKE, the fourth Master's Intercession

Know, great Sir, said Malquidrake to him, that there formerly lived in this city an old knight, who married a young lady, who complained to her mother, that she was unhappy in the marriage of this old man, designing to open her case to some priest. - From this her mother persuaded her, urging her to try his temper. The means she used were, to cut down the finest plant in the garden, and put a fire under it. Another time, she dashed out the brains of his favourite hound. And, lastly, when he and his friends were sitting at dinner, she threw all the dishes from off the table. Yet, with her excuses he seemed satisfied: and that morning she intended to go to the priest, he brought a surgeon into the chamber, commanded her to rise and be bled; whereat she began to entreat: but, said he, Your mad blood must be les out, and if you refuse that, I will have your heart's blood. - Upon this she permitted him to bleed her in both arms, till she fainted away: But, reviving, she sent for her mother, and told her his usage. The mother, being glad to hear this correction, said, that old men's revenge was sure, though slow; asking how she liked the priest? The devil take the priest, said she, I'll strive to please none but my husband. The emperor, hearing this, sent to spare his son. - The empress, understanding it, came and said, My lord, over this city ruled Octavius, who being troubled with the rebellion of his subjects, ordained his magician to devise a way how he might know, at any time, the state of the provinces: Upon which Virgilius[5] the most crafty of them, raised a tower, and placed in it as many images as provinces, and, in the hand of each, a bell, which, by the secret instinct of magic, rung out if any revolt happened in the province it was assigned guardian of so that the citizens instantly arriving suppressed the foes ere they could make head; which being known to the tributary nations, desirous to cast off the Roman yoke, they devised how to destroy the tower; which, after a long debate, was undertaken by four knights: who bringing great treasurer, hid it in four places near the walls of the city; and entering it, pretended to be south-sayers, and would discover hidden treasure. Which being known to the emperor, he sent for them, who pretending to dream, discovered the treasure they had hid. At last they pretended to dream, that under the tower lay a great treasure, and, if the emperor would permit, they would take it out; to which he consented. Whereupon they undermined the tower; and, at break of day, left the city, and were out of sight before it fell, At which the citizens being grieved, came to the emperor and acquainted him with it, and, understanding, that through his covetousness the mischief befel them, they carried him to the market-place, and poured melted gold down his throat, and buried him. The enemy soon after came upon the town, and took it; and destroying the inhabitants, took all their riches. The empress then demanded if he knew the meaning? Who replied in the negative. Well then, said she, the tower with the images signify your body, with its intellectual faculties; as long as they remain strong, and on a good foundation, you are safe; but if you give yourself up to the flattery of the masters, you must expect to fall. Rather than so, said he, they shall perish with my son.

CHAPTER VII

Josephus, the fifth Master's Intercession

DREAD Sir! may I beg your attention to the following example? Hippocrates, a famous physician, took to assist him his cousin Galenius,[6] who soon became more expert than he: Whereat, he endeavoured to hide from him his art, though in vain; for his prompt wit supplied other defects: So that sending him to visit great persons in their sickness, he ever cured them; which created such jealousies in Hippocrates, that he killed and buried him. But he falling sick, ordered his scholars to fill a cask of water, which they did; and, though an hundred holes were bored in it, yet none would issue hence: whereupon he said, he was a dead man; for, as no water came out of the herbs to cure his disease; but if his cousin had been alive he could have cured him: thus complaining, he died. For this example said the emperor, my son shall not die.

The empress hearing of this repreve, came and said: Great Sir, when the King of the Goths invaded Rome, he had a steward named Goadus: when one evening being merry with wine, he ordered him to bring him a beautiful woman, and he would have a great reward. Whereupon the steward compelled his wife to lye with the king, bargaining for a thousand pieces of silver, and the lady to depart ere morning. To this the king consented; she was brought, and the king enjoyed her: when, before day, the husband came, and entreated his lord to dismiss her; the king refused, saying, she pleased him so well, that she should sleep with him longer. Whereat he being much disturbed, told him she was his wife, and that for lucre he had forced her to his arms: At which the king, moved to anger, bade him depart on pain of death, which he did; and the king maintained his wife as his own. For this example, said the emperor, my son shall die to-morrow.

CHAPTER VIII

CLEOPHAS the sixth Master's Intercession

CLEOPHAS, came and said. There lived in this city a knight, who married a very beautiful lady, whose voice was so charming, that she ravished the heaven. One day as she sat singing with the casement open, three favourite knights of the emperor passed by, who were all much taken with her voice and person. They each took convenient times (without acquainting one another) to treat about enjoyment; to which she seemingly consented, in consideration, as she was but poor, they brought a hundred florins a-piece; and she appointed them to come singly at different times and she would receive them. Which done, she acquainted her husband, advising him to stand with sword drawn, and, as they entered, to kill them; which he performed, and taking away their money, threw their bodies into the sea. Soon after, the knight and his lady quarrelled, and he striking her, she cried out, in the hearing of many, O you monster! will you kill me, as you did the three knights ? They being missed created a suspicion; upon which they were both seized, confessed the fact, and were afterwards executed. - Then said the emperor, my son shall not die.

Upon this the empress came and said, My lord, In Armenia reigned a king, who had a beautiful wife, on whom he doated, and that none other might enjoy her, he confined her in a castle, and kept the keys himself. - The queen after four days confinement, dreamed she saw a knight who was enamoured with her, and she no less with him. Now, there was a knight who had heard of her beauty, and left his country to see her; but finding she was confined, rode about the castle hoping she might look out at the window, and he find means to discover his passion. Not long did his expectation fail, for the lady beholding him, concluded he was the man she beheld in her dream; and as he daily frequented the place, she took an opportunity to drop letter, which he took up and departed, consulting with himself how he might answer her expectations, which he determined thus: That he would insinuate himself into the king's favour; which he did by his great wisdom in state affairs, insomuch that the king made him steward of his household; and, accordingly, ordered an house to be built adjoining to the castle for him, through the building of which the knight contrived to cut the wall, and to make a private way into the castle; and then for secrecy slew the workmen. On his entering, he was joyfully received by the queen, who permitted him to take his fill of love, giving him the ring the king gave her on the wedding day; which the king noticed, as he slept in his presence. He perceived the discovery, feigned sick, and obtained licence to retire, conveying the ring to her again, ere the king came to enquire for it; Nay, he often brought her to the king's table, pretending she was a lady of his acquaintance, whom he intended shortly to wed. - The king earnestly looking, said, Well, if I had not the keys of the castle, I should almost swear it was my queen. Before he could go to prove it, she was returned, and in her usual dress. In the end, the knight desired the king to give him this lady in marriage, which he did, giving them great riches, with a ship to convey them to Greece where the knight had large possessions, and solemnly taking leave, they set sail; at which time the king set his eyes after them till out of sight, and afterwards went to divert himself with the queen; but coming into the castle, behold she was fled! He, suspecting the scheme, fell into great lamentations. - Even so, said she, will it befal you, if you thus give way to your masters. To prevent the like, said the emperor, they, with my son, to-morrow shall die.

CHAPTER IX

DIOCLES, the seventh Master's Intercession

The seventh master, named Diocles, came and said, Know Sir, that in Ephesus lived a knight who married a lady, upon whom he doated, that he could not endure her out of his sight: but playing at chess, and he holding a pen-knife in his hand; she hit her finger against it, which the knight seeing, fell into a swoon, and gave up the ghost: Whereupon, she staid mourning by his tomb. So her friends built her a house nigh to it, to mourn in. - Now, when a malefactor was to be hanged, it was the law of the country, that the sheriff should watch him on the gallows the ensuing night. The sheriff, discovering a light in the house of the above widow, came thither to warm himself, and, on return, found the thief stolen: Whereat, he concluded to go back to the widow, and desire her to put him in a way what to do. Upon this, she, pausing, told him, that, as the price of his love, she would put him in a way what to do, which was this: A few days ago, says she, my lord was buried; take and hang him up instead of the thief. But, said the sheriff, the thief had lost his eyes, teeth, and stones; as, likewise, in being taken, received a wound on his head. It is in your power to serve my lord so, said she. Nay, said he, not I. Then, said she, for the love of you I will perform it: And, taking a sword, she accordingly did it! So they dragged him to the gallows, and hanged him up. After which, she very urgently demanded of the sheriff to fulfil his promise. But he replied, O thou wickedest of women, how couldst thou be so cruel to the dead body of thy husband? Therefore, I will keep my word and not marry while thou livest. And with that drew his sword and slew her. - Then, said the master, you have understood what I related? To which he replied, Full well: and am of the opinion she was the worst of women; therefore, for the words of a woman, my son shall not die.

CHAPTER X

The PRINCE'S Complaint of the Empress

The seventh day the masters brought the prince to the emperor, who said, Hail, royal father, heaven can witness the falsity of the accusation laid against me; for instead of my having tempted the chastity of the empress; it was she that tempted me to lewdness with her, which I refused; and, because I would not speak, the planets having threatened my life, if in seven days I spoke one word, she fell into a rage and accused me: Nor is she nice in her honour, for, under the cover of a female garment, she keeps a youth to supply your place: and send for her attendants, and I will make it appear. At this the emperor ordered them all to be called in, and the person the prince pitched on proved to be a man, who confessed he had lain with the empress several times. This so enraged the emperor, that he cast them into prison, and the prince told the following story.

In Palestine lived a knight, who had one son, whom he held in high esteem; and for his noble accomplishments, caused him to be taught all the arts and sciences: in which being perfected, he sent for him, to come home. And as he sat at dinner, a nightingale sang sweetly; at which the knight said, Ah! how sweet a song is this! could any one but interpret it. To which the youth answered that he would undertake it, if he would not be displeased: but his father commanded him to interpret it. Then, said the youth, the bird, in her song, expressed that I would be a great lord; and that my father would hold the water, and my mother a towel, to wash my hands. - Whereupon the father growing angry, took him up, and running to the sea, and cast him in, where he swam to an uninhabited island, where he stayed three or four days, till a ship passing, took him up, and sold him to a duke in Egypt, who finding him wise, made him ruler of his house. It happened the king of the country was troubled with the cry of three ravens, and demanded of the wise men the cause, but they could not resolve him; therefore, he proclaimed, that if any could tell the meaning, or cause the noise to cease, he should have his daughter to wife, and the kingdom after his decease. Upon this, Alexander (the youth's name) went to the king, saying, that the ravens were the two old ones and their young one, the male declaring it was his right, seeing he had fed him in the time of famine, when the female, who flew into a far country to shift for herself, had left him to perish. - When, on the other side, the female alledged, she had taken pains, in laying the egg and brooding it; wherefore, the young one appertained to her. And now, O King, said Alexander, they come to you to decide the controversy; give judgement, and then the ravens shall trouble you no more - Then, replied the king, it seems good to me, that the young one abide with the male. And on his saying this, the ravens took wing and returned no more - The monarch thus delivered, confirmed his promise, and advanced Alexander to places of dignity. Alexander travelled to Rome, and there became carver to Titus, whose daughter became in love with him; but his heart being in Egypt, Lodowick was sent in his stead, and Alexander sailed into Egypt; but Guido discovering the intrigue of Lodowick and the emperor's daughter, sent him a challenge, who enraged Alexander; but he, being to celebrate the nuptials, sent Lodowick to celebrate them in his place, on condition that he would not rifle the princess of her virginity. Alexander arrived at court: The emperor supposing him to be Lodowick, and the list being ready, the combatants entered, and, after a fierce fight, Alexander cut off his foe's head, and sent it to the princess. The emperor highly extolled him; but he, saying his father was sick, took his leave and went back to Egypt. Sometime after, Alexander was made king of that country; and visiting his father and mother, one day, before dinner, according to the interpretation he had given of the bird's language, his father brought the basin and his mother the towel; but he refused to let them hold either, commanding his servants to do it. Dinner being ended, he asked them, how many children they had? They said none. Had you ever any? said the king. Alas! said the father, we had one son, but he was drowned long ago! Well, look you to it, said the king, for if I find it otherwise, you must expect no mercy. Then they fell upon their knees, and confessed the whole matter; which the king, mildly raising them from the ground, made a discovery of himself to them.

Upon hearing this story, the emperor resigned to government to his son Dioclesian; who demanded justice on the empress and her paramour; the former being burned and the latter hanged and quartered. And the emperor dying soon after, left his son in full possession of the empire.

FINIS

Notes on the Texts

Guy of Warwick (Prose)

1. The text of this chapbook is that of the abridged version of Samuel Smithson's original twenty-four page chapbook. It is identical, with the exception of a few minor verbal details, to the text printed by Dicey at Aldermary Churchyard, Bow in the 1740s and edited in facsimile by V.E. Neuburg (*The Penny Histories* (London, 1968). On the relationship between this shorter text and other *Guy of Warwick* chapbooks see R.S. Crane, 'The Vogue of Guy of Warwick from the Close of the Middle Ages to the Romantic Revival', *Publications of the Modern Language Association of America*, 30 (1915), pp. 171-4.

2. Probably not a misprint as Dicey's text shares this reading, though Ashton, (*Chapbooks of the Eighteenth Century* (London, 1882) has emended to 'prowess' which is the more obvious word.

3. It is tempting to think that Alexander Pope's 'Which Jews might kiss and Infidels adore' (*Rape of the Lock*, II, 8) is a memory of this phrase. Pope would almost certainly have read chapbooks as a child and any chapbook reader would have come across *Guy of Warwick*.

4. Galen was a second-century medical authority much respected in the Middle Ages.

5. Probably a misprint.

6. Dicey gives 'balm'.

7. Dicey gives 'raging'.

8. This sentiment surely reinforces Guy's quest to establish his status through chivalric prowess.

9. Throughout the text we are invited to see Guy as a hero who is particularly English.

10. Dicey gives 'meditate'.

11. It is instructive to compare this passage with the relevant stanza in Samuel Rowlands's poem:
Ev'n so this gentle creature deals with him,
For that same benefit which he hath done;

> Although by nature cruel, fierce and grim,
> Yet like a Spaniel by his horse did run;
> Continuing for many days with great desire,
> Till extream hunger forc'd him to retire.
> (F2ᵛ-F3ʳ)

12. The Guy of Warwick relics were the centre of an early modern tourist attraction at Warwick Castle throughout the seventeenth century. John Evelyn recorded his visit there on 3 August 1654 in his usual dry fashion:

> We pass'd next through Warwick, & saw the Castle
> which is built on an eminent rock ... Here they shew
> us Sir Guys greate two-handed Sword, Staff, horse-
> armes, Pott, & other reliques of that famous Knight
> errant ... Hence to Sir Guys Grott, where they say he
> did his penances, & dyed, & 'tis certainly a squalid
> den made in the rock croun'd yet with venerable
> Oakes, & respecting a goodly streame, so as were it
> Improv'd as it might be, 'twere capable of being
> Render'd one of the most romantique & pleasant
> places imaginable: neere this we were shown his
> Chapell, and gigantic statue hewn out of the solid
> Rock ... The next place was Coventry ... At going forth
> the Gate they shew us the bone or rib of a Wild-
> boare said to have been kild by Sir Guy, but which
> I take to be the chine of a Whale.
> (*Diary*, pp. 345-6)

See Crane, 'The Vogue of Guy of Warwick', pp. 168-9 for details of other visitors. Copland's print (1560s) also records the tradition: 'In Warwick the truth there ye shall see / In arras wrought full craftily' (5973-4).

13. This episode has much in common with similar adventures of another chapbook hero Jack the Giant Killer.

14. This pious observation is a good example of the ways in which chapbooks served many of the needs of their readership. The overtly scriptural moralism enables the text to be read as improving rather than merely entertaining.

15. The topography here is accurate as there is a Morn Hill near Winchester. Smithson follows Rowlands in setting the encounter at 'Hide Mead'. These events are still recorded on a plaque in the ruins of Hyde Abbey in Winchester. It may be valuable to

compare these events as recounted by Smithson with the text edited above:

Upon this, mighty Colbron singles himself from
the Danes, and entered into Hide-mead, near
Winchester, breathing out venemous Words, calling
the English cowardly Dogs, and that he would
make their Carcases meat for Crows and Ravens.
Is now, said Colbron, all your English Courage
become so timerous that you dare not fight? What
might boasting hath there been in foreign
Nations of these English Cowards, as if they had
done deeds of Wonder, who now like Foxes hide
their Heads saying, It is good to sleep in a
whole Skin.

(Crane, 'The Vogue of Guy of Warwick', p. 173)

Guy of Warwick (Verse)

1.   I have not been able to trace the source of this quotation. Chapbooks are frequently adorned with claims for their moral utility (see *The Seven Wise Masters*) though a citation of this sort is unusual and demonstrates a difference between the English and the American public.
2.   Misprint.
3.   Word illegible.

The Seven Champions of Christendom

1.   The use of the fall of Troy as a historical reference point is not unusual in medieval literature. The most celebrated example may be found in the opening lines of *Sir Gawain and the Green Knight*.
2.   A 'faulchion' is a kind of curved sword.
3.   The description of the fight with the dragon, especially the detail of the monster's brass scales relates back to *Bevis of Hampton* via Johnson's *Seaven Champions*, and has been retained in Slasher's speech in the Mummers' Plays:

My head is made of iron,
My body is made of steel,
My arms and legs of beaten brass,

No man can make me feel.
(Chambers, *The English Folk Play*, p. 178)

The role of chapbooks in the stimulation and dissemination of folk drama is beyond the scope of this book but see bibliography for some studies of the topic.

4.   This remarkable example of law-abiding citizenry is the sort of episode that might lead commentators to suspect that chapbooks represented a deliberate attempt to instil a spirit of docility into the rural poor.

5.   The reading is correct but one might suspect that Iudia might be more accurate. The famous textual crux in Shakespeare's *Othello*: 'Like the base Indian / Iudean threw a pearl away' springs readily to mind.

6.   At this point the printer switches to a smaller fount.

7.   This incident surely owes much to the romance of *Chevalere Assigne* or *Helyas* (see introduction). The probable debt of *The Seven Champions* to this text has not, to my knowledge, ever been investigated.

8.   The trade list at the end of the chapbook is particularly fascinating as it is richly suggestive of the close relationship between printers, booksellers, chapmen and the reading public. Here Cotton and Eddowes are advertising chapbooks which, presumably, they have both printed themselves and bought in from other sources. The list is a familiar one to students of chapbooks and the vast majority of titles also appear on the list of 'penny histories' which Cluer Dicey and Richard Marshall, perhaps the most celebrated of chapbook dealers, published in 1744 (see V.E. Neuburg, *A Chapbook Bibliography* (London, 1970), pp. 75-80). The list gives a very fair sample of the main genres of chapbooks (see introduction above) and a sense of what might be available in a small town. It may well be that the reference to 'Travellers' is to chapmen: certainly the Dicey/Marshall list was aimed primarily at pedlars rather than the general public. The titles may be described as follows:

i   *The Academy of Compliments*: probably a conduct book giving guidance in etiquette, especially in matters of courtship. This was a minor chapbook genre which included chapbooks giving series of sample letters illustrative of the progress of love affairs. There is, for example, a chapbook entitled *A Collection of Love-Letters to which is added The History of Sylvia*. This was printed by S. Garridge, who was active in Worcester 1758-1768, and gives not only sample letters but also a narrative of the affair. Looking at this chapbook one is forcibly reminded of Samuel Richardson's apprenticeship to the chapbook publisher John Wild (see introduction). A chapbook entitled *Valentine Writer* was listed some time between 1808 and 1820 as forming part of the stock of the Cheney family who were printers at Banbury (see Neuburg, *Chapbook Bibliography*, pp. 80-1 for the full Cheney list).

ii   *Captain Hind*: this is a rogue biography. Hind was a notorious seventeenth-century highwayman.

iii   *Robinson Crusoe*: self-explanatory.

iv   *Seven Champions*: self-explanatory.

v   *Courtier and Tinker*: this chapbook is not on Dicey and Marshall's list. It is the popular and witty story of the encounter between two men of different social status. This story was still being used in the eighteenth century and L. Colley (*Britons* (London, 1992), p.233) recounts the following anecdote of a meeting between a farmer and George III: 'The farmer grown familiar asked the gentleman, as he thought, if he had seen the King: and being answered in the affirmative, the farmer said "Our neighbours say he's a good sort of man, but dresses very plain." "Aye," said his Majesty, "as plain as you see me now," and rode on.'

vi   *Cookery Book*: self-explanatory.

vii   *Dreams and Moles*: a chapbook explaining the significance of the placing of moles and the interpretation of dreams. This chapbook would have included advice and spells concerning love and marriage.

viii   *Friar Bacon*: the traditional story best known in Greene's dramatised version but treated very much as a jest book in chapbook accounts.

ix   *Fairy Tales*: presumably the same title as that listed by Dicey and Marshall as *Fairy Stories*. Neuburg gives a facsimile of this in *The Penny Histories*. It contains 'The Blue Beard and Florina', 'The King of the Peacocks and Rosetta' and a 'New Song entitled the Fairies Dance'.

x   *Friar and Boy*: a very popular jest book and the first example here of a two part (i.e. two volume) chapbook.

xi   *Fortunatus*: adventures magical and humourous of the eponymous hero.

xii   *Fortune Book*: not in Dicey and Marshall's list. Another conduct book giving advice on courtship and various other matters from divination by moles and dreams through to cures for drunkenness and toothache.

xiii   *Guy of Warwick*: self-explanatory.

xiv   *Honest John and Loving Kate*: not in Dicey and Marshall's list. The description of a rural love affair: essentially another conduct chapbook.

xv   *Jack Horner*: a jest book.

xvi   *Jack and Giants*: a two-part version of the enormously popular chapbook *Jack the Giant Killer*.

xvii   *King and Cobler*: see *Courtier and Tinker* (above). An enormously popular chapbook usually associated with King Henry VIII.

xviii   *Lawrence Lazy*: a jest book.

xix   *Mother Bunch*: folk prophecy.

xx   *Mother Shipton*: folk prophecy.

xxi   *Patient Grissell*: the traditional story best known through Chaucer's 'Clerk's Tale'.

xxii   *Parents best Gift*: religious.

xxiii *Preparation for Heaven*: self-explanatory, not in Dicey and Marshall's list.

xxiv   *Riddles*: self-explanatory, not in Dicey and Marshall's list.

xxv   *Robin Hood*: self-explanatory.

xxvi   *Sir Richard Whittington*: self-explanatory.

xxvii *Tom Thumb*: self-explanatory with strong elements of jest book.

xxviii *Tom Tram*: jest book.

xxix   *Valentine and Orson*: self-explanatory.

Parismus

1.   The omission of letters is a fairly common typographical error in *Parismus*, which, as will be seen from the illustrations, has been printed relatively carelessly with what looks like a rather worn fount. The initial 's' of this word is struck as an inverted capital.

2.   Although this sentence is not strictly euphuistic it does give some sense of Forde's debt to the elaborate style popular after the publication of John Lyly's novel *Euphues* in 1578. The full euphuistic style which depends on lengthy and quasi-proverbial periphrases can hardly be reproduced in chapbook form, but Forde's style is so dependent on it that it could hardly be removed by mere abridgement.

3.   Terrace.

4.   Misprint. The composition has gone badly wrong here. The text reads 'Wind-mn-sick' with a lineal break after the 'n' (actually an inverted 'u').

5.   By the time this chapbook was printed the masque had died out as a form of aristocratic entertainment in England. However,

during the reigns of Elizabeth I, James I and Charles I it formed a very important element in the rituals of the court. The description gives a good idea of what a masque was like, especially as it shows both the participation in the entertainment of courtiers who were not professional actors or dancers, and the way in which masque could be used to convey symbolic and private messages to sections of the audience or even to individuals within it.

6.   Both misprints. The compositor has left a lineal break after the initial 'a' of 'about'.

7.   Allied.

8.   Misprint. The text reads 'in-toher' with a lineal break following the hyphen.

9.   Pullet.

10.   Trainbands or Trained Bands were militia units especially associated with the London citizenry during the seventeenth century.

11.   In battle order.

12.   The act of lowering the lance in readiness for an attack.

13.   Episodes which are analogous to the life of Parismenos in the wood and which mirror his innate understanding that he was born to better things are not uncommon in medieval romance and are probably related to the 'Great Fool' motif which has been noted elsewhere. The most celebrated example in Middle English may be found in the romance of *Percyvell of Gales*.

14.   See *Guy of Warwick* for the association of lions and knights.

Valentine and Orson

1.   The *Valentine and Orson* chapbook printed by Dicey and reproduced by Ashton in his *Chapbooks of the Eighteenth Century* adds the following couplet:
       And if with Caution you will read it thro'
       'Twill both instruct thee and Delight thee too.
       It is doubtful that many of the readers of this chapbook would have picked up this allusion to Horace. In the notes below some further interesting variants are given between the two texts but the very many small verbal and formal variations are not noted.

2.   The Dicey chapbook gives 'impudence' but 'imprudence' is a credible, if unusual, form in this context.

3.   The episode where children are progressively stolen by wild animals crops up in the Middle English romances. See, for example, *Sir Isumbras*.

4.   The motivation of King Pepin here is hard to follow due to the highly compressed language. Twins are often seen as a sign of marital infidelity in medieval literature. See for example, the romance of *Octavian*.

5.   The Dicey chapbook gives 'Giant' here.

6.   'Orson' literally means 'bear's son' so the folk-etymology is, strictly, incorrect.

7.   Orson is here playing the part of the 'Great Fool'. This role is common in romance and is often played by heroes either in disguise or in ignorance of their true noble nature. Examples of these types can be found in the romances of *Havelok the Dane* and *Ipomedon*. In chapbooks the type is also common - *Tom Hickathrift* is probably the best known example.

8.   A misprint for 'Acquitain'.

9.   An enchanted head of brass which can speak the future is also found in the chapbook of *Friar Bacon*.

10.   A similar motif is also found in Chaucer's 'Squire's Tale'.

11.   As in *Guy of Warwick* there is here a balancing of the secular and religious duties of knighthood and kingship.

12.   See *Guy of Warwick*: the attraction of *Valentine and Orson* as a chapbook must surely, in part, be due to its highly recognisable narrative structure.

13.   The Dicey chapbook adds the following: 'and his soul to the immortal deities of whose
      attributes it had a true resemblance.'

The Seven Wise Masters

1.   Misprint. The chapbook is, for the most part, carefully printed, though the type is somewhat worn; 'o's in particular are often very poorly struck.

2.   Misprint for 'intent'.

3.   This is a common tale. Probably the best known version of it in the British Isles is the one which features the Welsh Prince Llewelyn ap Gruffudd and his hound Gelert.

4.   A version of this story may be found in Boccaccio's *Decameron*, Day Seven, Tale Four.

5. By the Middle Ages a significant body of story and legend had built up around the Latin poet Virgil. These tales invested him with considerable magical powers. An English version of these legends was printed by John Doesborcke at Antwerp in 1518 and this was reprinted *c*.1562 by William Copland. The Latin prose work *Dolopathos*, which dates from about 1190 and was translated into French is the earliest western European version of *The Seven Wise Masters* and in it Virgil plays the role of counsellor to the falsely accused Prince.

6. Hippocrates (fifth century BC) was the most celebrated of the Ancient Greek physicians, still revered as the founder of modern medical ethics. Galen was a second-century medical authority much cited in the Middle Ages.

Bibliography

This bibliography includes all works cited in the text and notes together with a selection of works relating to chapbooks, the chapbook printing industry and chapbook readers. It does not include references to individual chapbooks.

Ackroyd, P., *Blake* (London, 1995)

Altick, R.D., *The English Common Reader* (Berkeley, 1963)

Anderson, R., *The Printed Image and the Transformation of Popular Culture 1760–1860* (Oxford, 1991)

Anglo, S. (ed.), *Chivalry in the Renaissance* (Woodbridge, 1990)

Armistead, G. and Silvermann, J., (eds), *The Judaeo-Spanish Chapbooks of Yacob Abraham Yona* (Berkeley, 1971)

Ashton, J., *Chapbooks of the Eighteenth Century* (London, 1882)

Axon, W.E.A., 'Some Twentieth-Century Italian Chapbooks', *The Library*, new series, 5 (1904), pp. 239–55

Bamford, S., *Early Days* (London, 1849)

Barber, G., 'Francis Douce and Popular French Literature', *Bodleian Library Record*, 14 (1993), pp. 397–428

Barron, W.R.J., *Medieval English Romance* (London, 1987)

Blake, N.F., 'Lord Berners: A Survey', *Medievalia et Humanistica*, 2 (1971), pp. 119–32

Blake, N.F., 'William Caxton's Chivalric Romances and the Burgundian Renaissance in England', *Essays and Studies*, 57 (1976), pp. 1–10

Blamires, D., 'An English Chapbook Version of the "Eaten Heart" Story', *Folklore*, 104 (1993), pp. 99–104

Bland, D.S., *Chapbooks and Garlands in the Robert White Collection* (Newcastle, 1956)

Bloom, C. (ed.), *Jacobean Poetry and Prose* (London, 1988)

Borrow, G., *Lavengro* (Oxford, 1982)

Boswell, J., *Boswell's London Journal*, ed. W.A. Pottle (London, 1950)

Bowles and Carver, *Catchpenny Prints* (New York, 1970)

Bradley, W., 'Eighteenth Century Chapbooks and Broadsides', *The American Chapbook*, I (1904)

Braudel, F., *The Mediterranean in the Age of Philip II* (London, 1975)

Brewer, J., *The Common People and Politics 1750–1790* (Cambridge, 1986)

Brissenden, R.F. (ed.), *Studies in the Eighteenth Century* (Canberra, 1968)

Brown, R.D., *Knowledge is Power* (Oxford, 1989)

Burke, P., *Popular Culture in Early Modern Europe* (London, 1978)

Burke, P., 'The "Discovery" of Popular Culture', in R. Samuel (ed.), *People's History and Socialist Theory* (London, 1981), pp. 216–21

Burke, P., 'Chivalry in the New World', in S. Anglo, *Chivalry in the Renaissance* (Woodbridge, 1990), pp. 253–62

Capp, B., *Astrology and the Popular Press* (London, 1979)

Chambers, E.K., *The English Folk Play* (Oxford, 1933)

Chartier, R., *The Cultural Uses of Print in Early Modern France* (Princeton, 1987)

Clare, J., *Autobiographical Fragments*, ed. E. Robinson (Oxford, 1986)

Clark, J.C.L., *Notes on Chapman Whitcomb* (Lancaster, Mass., 1911)

Colley, L., *Britons* (London, 1992)

Crane, R.S., 'The Vogue of Guy of Warwick from the Close of the Middle Ages to the Romantic Revival', *Publications of the Modern Language Association of America*, 30 (1915), pp. 125–94

Cressy, D., *Bonfires and Bells* (London, 1989)

Cunningham, R.H., *Amusing Prose Chap-books* (London, 1889)

Darnton R., and Roche, D. (eds), *Revolution in Print* (Berkeley, 1989)

Darton, F.J.H., *Children's Books in England* (3rd ed., Cambridge, 1982)

Davidson, C.N. (ed.), *Reading in America* (Baltimore, 1989)

Davis, R., *Kendrew of York and his Chapbooks for Children* (York, 1988)

Deacon, G., *John Clare and the Folk Tradition* (London, 1983)

Dickson, A., *Valentine and Orson: A Study in Late Medieval Romance* (New York, 1929)

Doutrepont, G., *Les Mises en Prose des Epopées et Romans Chevaleresques* (Brussels, 1939)

Embley, C., and Walvin, J, (eds), *Artisans, Peasants and Proletarians 1760–1860* (London, 1985)

Evelyn, J., *Diary*, ed. E.S. de Beer (Oxford, 1959)

Farrell, D.E., 'The Origins of Russian Popular Prints and their Social Milieu in the Early Eighteenth Century', *Journal of Popular Culture*, 17 (1983), pp. 9–47

Feather, J., 'John Clay of Daventry: The Business of an Eighteenth-Century Stationer', *Studies in Bibliography*, 37 (1984), pp. 198–209

Federer, C.A., *Yorkshire Chapbooks* (London, 1899)

Fellows, J., Field, R., Rogers, G. and Weiss, J. (eds), *Romance Reading on the Book* (Cardiff, 1996)

Fellows, J., '*Bevis Redivivus*: the printed editions of *Sir Bevis of Hampton*', in J. Fellows, R. Field, G. Rogers and J. Weiss (eds), *Romance Reading on the Book* (Cardiff, 1996), pp. 251–68

Fergus, J., 'Eighteenth-Century Readers in Provincial England: The Customers of Samuel Clay's Circulating Library and Bookshop, 1770–1772', *Papers of the Bibliographical Society of America*, 78 (1984), pp. 155–213

Fergus, J. and Portner, R., 'Provincial Booksellers in Eighteenth-Century England: the Case of John Clay Reconsidered', *Studies in Bibliography*, 40 (1987), pp. 147–63

Friedman, J., *Miracles and the Pulp Press during the English Revolution* (London, 1993)

Gaskell, P., *A New Introduction to Bibliography* (Oxford, 1972)

Gering, C., *Notes on Printers* (London, 1900)

Gilmore, W.J., *Reading becomes a Necessity of Life* (Knoxville, 1989)

Good, D., *Catalogue of the Spencer Collection of Early Children's Books and Chapbooks* (Preston, 1967)

Gortschacher, W. and Klein, H. (eds), *Narrative Strategies in Early English Fiction* (Lewiston, 1995)

Gosse, E. (ed.), *Works of Samuel Rowlands* (Glasgow, 1880)

Hall, D.D., and Brown, R.D. (eds), *Printing and Society in Early America* (Worcester, Mass., 1983)

Harker, D., *Fakesong* (Milton Keynes, 1985)

Hart, J.D., *The Popular Book* (Berkeley, 1961)

Harvard College, *Catalogue of English and American Chapbooks and Broadside Ballads in Harvard College Library* (Cambridge, Mass., 1905)

Harvey, W., *Scottish Chapbook Literature* (Dundee, 1903)

Hayes, G.R., 'Anthony Munday's Romances of Chivalry', *The Library*, 4th series, 6 (1925), pp. 57–81

Helm, A., *The English Mummers' Play* (Woodbridge, 1981)

Hibbard, L.A., *Medieval Romance in England* (New York, 1924)

Hindley, C., *The Catnach Press* (London, 1869)

Hindley, C., *Curiosities of Street Literature* (Welwyn Garden City, 1969)

Hirsch, R.S.M., 'The Source of Richard Johnson's *Look on Me London*', *English Language Notes*, 13 (1975), pp. 107–13

Holcroft, T., *Hugh Trevor*, ed. S. Deanes (Oxford, 1973)

Houston, R.A., *Scottish Literacy and the National Identity* (Cambridge, 1985)

Hunter, J.P., *Before Novels* (London, 1990)

Hurlimann, B., *Three Centuries of Children's Books in Europe* (London, 1967)

Hutton, R., *The Rise and Fall of Merry England: the Ritual Year, 1400–1700* (Oxford, 1994)

Isaac, P.G., *William Davison of Alnwick* (Oxford, 1968)

Isaac, P.G., *Halfpenny Chapbooks by William Davison* (Newcastle, 1971)

Jaffee, D., 'Peddlers of Progress and the Transformation of the Rural North 1760–1860', *Journal of American History* (1991), pp. 515–35

James, L., *Fiction for the Working Man* (London, 1963)

James, L., *Print and the People* (Harmondsworth, 1978)

Johnson, R., *The History of Tom Thumbe*, ed. C. F. Buhler (Evanston, 1965)

Johnson, R., *The Most Pleasant History of Tom a Lincolne*, ed. R.S.M. Hirsch (New York, 1978)

Johnston, A., *Enchanted Ground* (London, 1964)

Joyce, P., *Democratic Subjects* (Cambridge, 1994)

Joyce, W.L., et al., *Printing and Society in Early America* (Worcester, Mass., 1983)

Kiefer, M., *American Children through their Books* (Philadelphia, 1948)

Klancher, J.P., *The Making of English Reading Audiences 1790–1832* (Madison, 1987)

Ladurie, J., *Love, Death and Money in the Pays d'Oc* (Harmondsworth, 1984)

Laqueur, T.W., *Religion and Sensibility* (New Haven, 1976)

Leary, L., *The Book-Peddling Parson* (Chapel Hill, 1984)

Leitch, R., ' "Here chapmen billies tak their stand": a pilot study of Scottish chapmen, packmen and pedlars', *Proceedings of the Society of Antiquarians of Scotland*, 120 (1990), pp. 173–88

Lindfors, B., 'Heroes and Hero-Worship in Nigerian Chapbooks', *Journal of Popular Culture*, 1 (1967), pp. 1–22

Lyle, E.B., 'A Checklist of Chapbooks Printed by William Scott of Greenock', *Bibliotheck*, 10 (1980), pp. 35–48

Mabbott, T.D., 'Two Chapbooks Printed by Andrew Steuart', *American Book Collector*, 3 (1932), pp. 325–28

MacGregor, G. (ed.), *The Collected Writings of Dougal Graham*, 2 vols (Glasgow, 1883)

McKerrow, R.B., *An Introduction to Bibliography for Literary Students* (Oxford, 1927)

McSparran, F. and Robinson, P.R. (eds), *Cambridge University Library MS Ff. 2. 38* (London, 1979)

Maidment, B., *The Poor House Fugitives* (Manchester, 1987)

Maidment, B., *Reading Popular Prints 1790–1870* (Manchester, 1996)

Mandrou, R., *De La Culture Populaire au dix-huitième siécle* (Paris, 1985)

Mish, C., 'Black Letter as a Social Discriminant', *Publications of the Modern Language Association of America*, 68 (1953), pp. 627–30

Neuburg, V.E., *A Chapbook Bibliography* (London, 1964, 2nd ed., London, 1970)

Neuburg, V.E., *The Penny Histories* (London, 1968)

Neuburg, V.E., 'The Diceys and the Chapbook Trade', *The Library*, 5th series, 24 (1969), pp. 221–31

Neuburg, V.E., *Popular Education in Eighteenth-Century England* (London, 1971)

Neuburg, V.E., *Popular Literature* (Harmondsworth, 1977)

Neuburg, V.E., 'Chapbooks in America', in C.N. Davidson (ed.), *Reading in America* (Baltimore, 1989), pp. 81–113

Norton, F.J. and Wilson E.M. (eds), *Two Spanish Verse Chapbooks* (Cambridge, 1969)

Nye, R., *The Unembarrassed Muse* (New York, 1970)

Obiechina, E.N., *Onitsha Market Literature* (London, 1972)

O'Connor, D., *Amadis de Gaulle* (New Brunswick, 1970)

Patchell, M., *The Palmerin Romances* (New York, 1947)

Pearsall, D. (ed.), *The Auchinleck Manuscript* (London, 1979)

Pearson, E., *Banbury Chapbooks* (Welwyn Garden City, 1970)

Percy, T., *Reliques of Ancient English Poetry* (London, 1765)

Pitcher, E.W., 'The Serial Publication and Collecting of Pamphlets 1790–1815', *The Library*, 5th series, 30 (1975), pp. 322–29

Porter, R., *English Society in the Eighteenth Century* (Harmondsworth, 1982)

Pottinger, D.T., *The French Book Trade in the Ancien Regime* (Cambridge, Mass., 1958)

Preston, M.J., Smith, M.G. and Smith, P.S., *An Interim Checklist of Chapbooks containing Traditional Play Texts* (Newcastle, 1976)

Ratcliffe, F.W., 'Chapbooks with Scottish Imprints in the Robert White Collection', *Bibliotheck*, 4 (1964), pp. 88–174

Reay, B., *Popular Culture in Seventeenth-Century England* (London, 1988)

Renold, P., 'William Rusher: A Sketch of his Life', *Cake and Cockhorse*, 11 (1991), pp. 218–28

Richardson, A., *Literature, Education and Romanticism* (Cambridge, 1994)

Rivers, I. (ed.), *Books and their Readers in Eighteenth-Century England* (Leicester, 1982)

Rogers, P., 'Classics and Chapbooks', in I. Rivers (ed.), *Books and their Readers in Eighteenth-Century England* (Leicester, 1982), pp. 27–46

Rogers, P., 'Defoe's *Tour* (1742) and the Chapbook Trade', *The Library*, 6th series, 6 (1984), pp. 275–79

Rogers, P., *Literature and Popular Culture in Eighteenth-Century England* (Brighton, 1985)

Roscoe, S., *John Newberry and his Successors* (Wormley, 1973)

Roscoe, S. and Brimmel, A., *James Lumsden and Son of Glasgow* (London, 1981)

Rowe, W. and Schelling, V., *Memory and Modernity* (London, 1991)

Rule, J., *The Labouring Classes in Early Industrial England 1750–1850* (London, 1986)

Salzmann, P., *English Prose Fiction, 1558–1700* (Oxford, 1985)

Samuel, R. (ed.), *People's History and Socialist Theory* (London, 1981)

Severs, J.B., *A Manual of the Writings in Middle English*, I (New Haven, 1967)

Schick, F.L., *The Paperbound Book in America* (New York, 1958)

Scribner, R.W., *For the Sake of Simple Folk* (Oxford, 1994)

Shepard, L., *John Pitts* (London, 1969)

Shepard, L., *The History of Street Literature* (Newton Abbot, 1973)

Shepard, L., *The Broadside Ballad* (Wakefield, 1978)

Simons, J., 'Medieval Chivalric Romance and Elizabethan Popular Literature' (unpubl. Ph.D. thesis, Exeter, 1982)

Simons, J., 'Open and Closed Books: a Semiotic Approach to the History of Jacobean Popular Romance', in C. Bloom (ed.), *Jacobean Poetry and Prose* (London, 1988), pp. 8–24

Simons, J. (ed.), *From Medieval to Medievalism* (London, 1992)

Simons, J., 'Medievalism as Cultural Process in Pre-industrial Popular Literature', *Studies in Medievalism*, 7(1995), pp. 5–21

Simons, J., 'Transforming the Romance: Some Observations on Early Modern Popular Narrative', in W. Gortschacher and H. Klein (eds), *Narrative Strategies in Early English Fiction* (Lewiston, 1995), pp. 273–88

Simons, J., 'Robert Parry's *Moderatus*: A Study in Elizabethan Romance, in J.Fellows, R. Field, G. Rogers and J. Weiss, *Romance Reading on the Book* (Cardiff, 1996), pp. 237–50

Simons, J., 'Irish Chapbooks in the Huntington Library', *Huntington Library Quarterly*, 57 (1995), pp. 359–65

Simpson, C.M., *The British Broadside Ballad and its Music* (New Brunswick, 1986)

Slack, P., *Rebellion, Popular Protest and the Social Order in Early Modern England* (Cambridge, 1984)

Society for the Diffusion of Useful Knowledge, *The Penny Magazine*, 1 (London, 1832)

Spufford, M., *Small Books and Pleasant Histories* (Cambridge, 1981)

Spufford, M., *The Great Reclothing of Rural England* (London, 1984)

Stockham, P., *Chapbooks* (London, 1976)

Storch, R.D., (ed.), *Popular Culture and Custom in Nineteenth Century England* (London, 1982)

Summerfield, G., *Fantasy and Reason: Children's Literature in the Eighteenth Century* (London, 1983)

Thackeray, W.M., *The Irish Sketch Book*, 2 vols (London, 1843)

Thelander, D.R., 'Mother Goose and her Goslings: The France of Louis XIV as Seen Through the Fairy Tale', *Journal of Modern History*, 54 (1982), pp. 467–96

Thomas, H., *Spanish and Portuguese Romances of Chivalry* (Cambridge, 1920)

Thompson, A.R., 'Chapbook Printers', *Bibliotheck*, 6 (1972), pp. 76–83

Thompson, E.P., *The Making of the English Working Class* (Harmondsworth, 1963)

Thompson, E.P., *Customs in Common* (Harmondsworth, 1991)

Thompson, F.M., *Newcastle Chapbooks* (Newcastle, 1969)

Thompson, R., 'Samuel Pepys Penny Merriments: A Checklist', *The Library*, 5th series, 31 (1976), pp. 223–34

Tiddy, E., *The English Mummers' Plays* (Chicheley, 1972)

Tsurumi, R., 'The Development of Mother Goose in Britain in the Nineteenth Century', *Folklore*, 101 (1990), pp. 28–35

Valenze, D., 'Prophecy and Popular Literature in the Eighteenth Century', *Journal of Ecclesiastical History*, 29 (1978), pp. 75–92

Vincent, D., *Bread, Knowledge and Freedom* (London, 1981)

Vincent, D., 'The Decline of the Oral Tradition in Popular Culture', in R.D. Storch (ed.), *Popular Culture and Custom in Nineteenth-Century England* (London, 1982), pp. 20–47

Vincent, D., 'Communication, Community and the State', in C. Embley and J. Walvin (eds), *Artisans, Peasants and Proletarians 1760–1860* (London, 1985), pp. 166–86

Vincent, D., *Literacy and Popular Culture 1750–1914* (Cambridge, 1989)

Ward, P., *Cambridge Street Literature* (Cambridge, 1978)

Wasserman, E.R., *Elizabethan Poetry in the Eighteenth Century* (Urbana, 1948)

Watt, T., *Cheap Print and Popular Piety 1550–1640* (Cambridge, 1991)

Webb, R.K., *The English Working Class Reader* (London, 1955)

Weiss, H.B., 'The Charms of Chapbooks', *American Book Collector*, 1 (1932) pp. 166–9

Weiss, H.B., 'Alexander Wilson as a Chapbook Author', *American Book Collector*, 2 (1932), pp. 218–9

Weiss, H.B., 'Chapman Whitcombe', *The Book Collector's Packet*, 3 (1939), pp. 1–3

Weiss, H.B., *A Book about Chapbooks* (Trenton, 1942)

Weiss, H.B., 'American Chapbooks 1722–1842', *Bulletin of the New York Public Library*, 49 (1945), pp. 491–8 and 587–96

Wiles, R.M., 'Middle Class Literacy in Eighteenth–Century England: Fresh Evidence', in R.F. Brissenden (ed.), *Studies in the Eighteenth Century* (Canberra, 1968), pp. 49–66

Wilkomm, H.W., *Uber Richard Johnson's Seaven Champions of Christendome* (Berlin, 1911)

Williams, F.B., Jr., 'Richard Johnson's Borrowed Tears', *Studies in Philology*, 34 (1937), pp. 186–90

Wolf, E., II, *The Book Culture of a Colonial American City* (Oxford, 1988)

Wood, M., *Radical Satire and Print Culture* (Oxford, 1994)

Worrall, D., *Radical Culture* (Brighton, 1992)

Wright, L.B., *Middle-Class Culture in Elizabethan England* (Chapel Hill, 1935)

Zipes, J., *Beauties, Beasts and Enchantments* (New York, 1991)